The Hemlock Aperture

Steve Hooley

For Mark & Susie

Steve Hooley

For we wrestle not against flesh and blood, but against principalities, against powers, against the rulers of the darkness of this world, against spiritual wickedness in high places.

—EPHESIANS 6:12 (KJV)

For Leighton, Regan, Averie, Brooklyn, Ethan, Lillian, and Marian
who inspired this story.

<u>Acknowledgements</u>

Samantha Holland for her help with the magic spells translation
and her incredible Shawnee Dictionary, <u>Say It in Shawnee</u>

First readers and their suggestions – Cindy, Tessa, Ben, Andy,
Jim, and Ev

Lisette Hiatt and her honors English class beta readers
Lanny, Caitlin, Miriam, Malcolm, David,
Anastasia, Madison, and Olivia
For their middle grade and YA perspective and advice

Tom Carrig and students Leanna and Nicole
of the Ohio Hi-Point Career Center
Graphic Design Department
For a wonderful cover

Author – Steve Hooley
Visit my website at www.SteveHooleyWriter.com

Printed in the United States of America

First Printing: January 2019
Cedar Crest Creations

ISBN-13 978-1-0968805-7-8

Contents

Chapter One

Once Upon a Time

$\mathcal{N}$estled in the high hills of western Ohio near the headwaters of the magic Mad River, there lies an enchanted forest called Cedar Heights. Within that forest lives a family of magicians. Grandma and Grandpa are lovingly called Gram and Gramps. Gram and Gramps' five children have left their wizarding ways and gone off to live in the normal world, but every summer the seven grandchildren come back to Cedar Heights to explore the forest and steep themselves in the magic that permeates the wooded farmland.

One spring a curious phenomenon sprouted in the back corner of Cedar Heights. Now, it was normal for new saplings to burst from the warm earth each spring and regenerate a constantly growing and dying forest. But this young tree was different. It appeared at first to be a cedar tree, which were abundant in Cedar Heights, but then it morphed into a hemlock tree, of which there were no others in the forest. But stranger still was the way the little tree grew. Fast. It reached upward at an alarming speed, reaching ten feet in the two months before Gramps found it.

Its bark turned slate-gray, instead of the brown-gray that would have been normal for a hemlock. Its needles arranged themselves on the tiny branches in the familiar graceful palm-like shape that invited touch, but they wore the glossy colors of white and black, like painted fingernails. Even more alarming was the fruit. Rather than the normal small pine cones that would develop on an older tree, this precocious plant began growing apples, or what appeared to be apples, in all shades of gray.

As this freak pushed upward, the ground around it receded into a circular basin, leaving only a little mound of bare earth protruding in the center where the hemlock grew. Grass and living vegetation escaped from the basin as the indentation dropped deeper and deeper. As the sterile basin grew, the rumblings began. The ground shook, a low-pitched groan rose from deep within the earth, and the basin became deeper and wider.

Finally, the hemlock began consuming living creatures within its reach. The earth shook, the rumble rose, and an aperture appeared out of a cloud of dust, suspended in midair beside the hemlock. This large opening had a round external shape with movable plates that could adjust the size of the internal opening, like a camera aperture. This gray hole tricked the eye with a fuzzy dust-like appearance, like a holographic image you could see through. Was it really there?

Trees on the perimeter of the basin were torn from their woodland home, roots and all, and with a mighty roar they popped through the aperture and into the abyss.

Birds and insects attracted to the unusual apples would swarm around the tree. With a quick rumble and a roar, the aperture would open like a camera shutter. A whoosh and a puff of gray dust sucked the winged visitors in, and the opening quickly closed and disappeared.

As the hungry hemlock's appetite grew, the basin became even larger and deeper, the rumbling became stronger and stronger, and the roar became louder and louder...until finally Gramps noticed.

By the time Gramps located the source of the commotion, the danger had become extreme. Standing at a safe distance, Gramps observed rabbits and squirrels being sucked into the aperture, then even full-grown deer appeared to jump from the perimeter of the basin and dive into the opening.

As Gramps watched and explored this unbelievably frightening development in the back of his forest, he told no one, hoping it would disappear. He didn't want a law enforcement and media circus trampling his enchanted forest. But when he saw people flash before him and disappear into the hole, he knew he had to take action.

The next day, while mesmerized by the man-eating hole, he felt an invisible fist clutch his chest and drag him toward the aperture. As he dangled over the edge of the basin, grasping desperately to a cedar tree with one hand, he barely escaped by using his magic wand in his other hand and breathing a quick frantic prayer.

Now it was clear. An evil threat to Cedar Heights was not only consuming the flora and fauna of the forest, but also had an appetite for him and his family.

Chapter Two

Man-Eating Hole

"Stay away from it!" said Gramps.

Bolt gaped at the largest, ugliest hole in the back of Cedar Heights he had ever seen, having no clue that this would be the beginning of the biggest adventure of his twelve-year-old life.

"I'm telling the two of you," said Gramps, staring at Bolt and Leighton, "because you're the two most likely to venture farthest from the house and explore the back of the forest."

Gramps stood beside his old dependable all-terrain vehicle, the orange Kubota. He called it "the Tiger." His old safari hat was crushed and twisted in his calloused hands. White hair, thinning on top, betrayed his seventy-something age, but everything else revealed work and vigor, from his muscular arms to his dirty jeans and work boots. And his dark piercing eyes left no doubt that he meant business.

The two boys looked at each other, gulped, then looked quickly back at the hole. Bolt had never heard such a stern warning from Gramps, except when the cousins were fighting and he had to yell to get their attention. Part of Bolt wanted to step back away from the danger. Gramps certainly was taking this seriously. But why, if it was so dangerous, had he even brought them here?

Just twenty minutes ago, when they had finished the first two prototypes of the barrel carts, Gramps had insisted that Bolt and Leighton accompany him on a trial run, pulling the carts behind the Tiger. The boys had hesitated. Not that they didn't want to go. They were always eager for a new adventure. They also looked for every opportunity, when Gramps wasn't around, to work on the turbo-levitators. But, to keep Gramps happy, they had hopped into their carts and headed into the forest, never expecting this.

Steve Hooley

As the short train of the Tiger and two barrel carts entered the forest, Gramps was strangely quiet. Why wasn't he looking back to admire their new project? They had turned each of the old fifty-five gallon oil barrels on its side and cut out a big oval hole. Then an axle and wheels were mounted underneath. Finally the inside of the barrel was outfitted with a steering wheel and seat. Just big enough for one passenger, each barrel cart was hooked to the cart in front and behind, making a train. Some people called them train carts. Gramps called them barrel carts. Bolt and Scout had a better idea. They would make them fly.

The canopy of trees reached across the trail, turning it into a living tunnel. Light flickered in shafts, penetrating the leaves and branches, spotting the floor of the trail below. Birds took flight and disappeared as they approached. Covered with rotting leaves, the soft ground cushioned the bouncing cart tires, dampened the sounds, and provided the pungent aroma of a woodland hideaway.

Ignoring Gramps' unusual quiet concentration, Bolt focused on the barrel carts and how the turbo-levitators would soon power them to rocket silently through the tunnels. Leighton also appeared to be studying his cart, no doubt preparing to race it.

Leighton, or "Scout" as Bolt called him, was always taking something apart to study or creating a new invention. He had his head under the dash, looking. Nothing showed but his thick dark brown hair. He looked up and smiled at Bolt. Thumbs up. Ah, he had solved another design problem with the turbo-levitators. His round black glasses and small stature fit his intellectual curiosity.

Bolt tapped his crutches that were fastened securely in the hooks on either side of his cart. He and Scout would soon be conducting a new kind of race, one that would be much more fun, faster, and more challenging than stick-hopping on crutches through the forest. Who knew where it might lead. He couldn't wait.

Gramps had headed straight for the back of the forest, then pulled to a stop in a large clearing beside a huge circular fence. The wire mesh was continuous. No gate or opening presented an entry point. Barbed wire along the top of the fence said stay out. Had Gramps built this?

Now he and Scout stood beside Gramps, not knowing whether to be frightened or to be excited about the biggest discovery Cedar Heights had ever presented. This was amazing. The fence kept them away from the edge of the hole. But from their vantage point the hole appeared to be a hundred feet across with a floating island in the middle. And on that island was growing one strange tree. Sod hung down into the hole around the edges, like a thick table cloth draped over a mysterious black vertical surface. Only, there was nothing there. The earth had disappeared, leaving a blackness that defied reality. Bolt so wanted to peer over that edge.

Scout looked at Gramps. "Can we climb the fence?" he said.

"No!" said Gramps. "That's why I brought the two of you here, to warn you and to help keep the rest of the gang away."

4

"What's so dangerous?" asked Bolt. Anything new was something that deserved exploring. It was just a big hole in the ground.

"That hole is growing," said Gramps, pointing at it with his hat. "It's getting wider and deeper. I've tossed a rope into it, and I haven't hit the bottom yet. If you were to fall in, you'd never be found." His eyes drilled into each boy.

Scout looked at Gramps with wide eyes. "Why don't you fix it?" he asked.

"Yeah," said Bolt, pulling out his pencil-size wand from his pocket. "You said these wands were to be used for good magic. Wouldn't fixing that hole be something good?"

Tears formed in Gramps eyes. "Some things are never understood and always beyond our control. We don't know the power or reason behind that hole. There are both good and evil influences that are stronger than the magic we can perform." he said, shaking his head with a worried look on his face. "Besides, I've already tried. Come on. Let's get back to the house." He turned and started walking toward the Tiger.

Bolt heard a deep rumbling noise. "What's that?" he asked Gramps, as he looked back. The noise was definitely coming from the hole and getting louder. A huge translucent camera aperture appeared from a cloud of dust beside the strange tree.

"Quick!" said Gramps. "Get into the carts." He began to trot.

The ground began to shake. Now this was getting scary. Bolt stick-hopped to his cart and jumped in. Scout was right behind him.

Dust began to billow from the hole in large puffs, like a subterranean smoke signal. He felt a lump in his throat. He wanted to see what was happening, but he also wanted to get away from this place as quickly as possible.

As the Tiger sputtered to a start and the carts began to pull away, Bolt looked back in time to see a huge oak at the edge of the opening start leaning into the hole. Then an explosive boom, like a cannon, thundered through the forest, and the tree shot into the aperture. The aperture disappeared into a cloud of dust. The boys jumped out of their carts and climbed into the Tiger with Gramps.

Chapter Three

The Magic World of Cedar Heights

*B*olt jumped out of bed, eager to get to Cedar Heights and discuss the big hole in the back of the forest. He had been awake all night thinking about this. Why should he be afraid of a hole in the ground? Of course it had belched and rumbled and even eaten a tree, but it was still just a hole. And man, that floating island with that crazy tree. That was weird. There had to be a way to explore it without being swallowed alive.

It was time to call a boys' club meeting. He needed to make sure that Scout didn't breathe a word of this to the girls. If they found out, they would be in the way. Regan and Lillian would look up magic spells in Gramps' old magic books. Averie would want to come along with the boys when they were trying to explore it. Yeah, he needed to get to Cedar Heights, like right now. Which reminded him of how hungry he was. And that reminded him of Gram's breakfasts.

He glanced at his watch. There was still time to make it if he hurried. After dressing quickly, he hustled out to the living room to grab his cell phone. As expected, Jack was already on the computer. Under his breath he always called his stepfather Jerk. It really fit. Only 8 o'clock, and Jerk was already hogging the computer, sitting sprawled out in the middle of the couch, playing his video games, and even on his second beer. Same shirt as yesterday. Bolt hopped behind him, sniffing. Yep, he hadn't showered, either.

Bolt wondered what his mom had ever seen in this bum. She was off working every day, trying to support them. Jerk claimed he was disabled. Disabled, my foot. He could certainly move when he chased Bolt out of the house.

Bolt turned back to the bedroom.

"Stay off the Wi-Fi," said Jerk, without even looking up. "You use too much band width. I'm trying to beat one of my buddies in Seattle, and I don't want you slowing down the computer."

Bolt knew that, but he couldn't resist aggravating him. "What's for breakfast?" he asked.

That got Jerk's attention. He looked up. "Since when did you ever eat here?" said Jerk. "Mama Gram always has your breakfast fixed, just the way you like it. I bet she butters your toast for you, you big baby. Now get out of here and quit disturbing me. And make sure you latch the door behind you. I don't want any more flies getting in."

"Well, maybe if you took a shower," muttered Bolt under his breath. He smiled as he looked in the mirror, trying to comb his unruly hair. He really should learn some of those spells from Regan and Lillian. It would be fun to make the computer go haywire and cause Jerk to totally lose control. Hmm.

He pushed down the spike of white hair on the top of his head, but it stood right back up. One spike of white in the middle of thick red hair. Mom said the delivery room exploded in white light from a lightning bolt the night he was born. His head, covered in blood, popped out just after midnight, Saint Patrick's Day. The nurses wanted to call him Ruddy, because of all the red blood and red hair. But Mom saw the white lightning rod spiking up in the middle and said his name would be Bolt.

He gave up and laid down the comb. Time to wake up Finklestein.

Bolt stick-hopped out the door, slamming it just hard enough to get Jerk's attention. It sure would be nice to have a real dad. He guessed that was part of the reason he enjoyed spending time at Gram and Gramps' house, or Cedar Heights, as they called it. They weren't really his Grandparents, but they insisted he call them Gram and Gramps. And they actually treated him just like one of the seven cousins. There was always a chair at the table for him, and Gram made it clear that he was expected. He glanced at his watch again. He'd better get moving. Just enough time to give old Mr. Finklestein some heartburn.

One house stood between Bolt's house and Cedar Heights, and that was Mr. and Mrs. Finklestein's house. Bolt had never set out to make enemies, but somehow Mr. Finklestein had learned to hate him. It might have had something to do with Bolt crossing his yard. There was no quick way around the Finklestein property, and it was only fifty yards across it. And even on crutches, Bolt could cover that distance quickly.

He remembered being in the hospital, when his weak legs were first evaluated. When the docs gave him crutches, he was soon racing them down the halls. One of the nurses said he looked like a grasshopper. The doc said, "No, he's a stickhopper." And soon he was stick-hopping, stick-sprinting, and now even stick-vaulting. Oh, he loved the challenges.

Well Mr. Finkelstein, or Mr. Fink, as Bolt called him, was finicky and crotchety. He kept his yard perfectly mowed, at least twice a week. Every blade in place. Any leaf that dared drop on the plush green carpet was picked up within the hour. And when Bolt began crossing the yard, Mr. Fink acted like it was a cardinal sin. Shoot, all he was doing was walking across the grass.

Well, at first Old Man Fink yelled and screamed at him. Now, Bolt could stick-sprint across that fifty yards on his crutches in seven seconds flat, so he didn't have to take the abuse very long. But when Mr. Fink built a fence, that's when the competition and the fun began. That fence was like high hurdles. Although weak, Bolt's legs were long, and he loved to swing up and over the fence, with his crutches trailing along behind him. And somehow he couldn't keep from yelling to make sure that Mr. Fink saw him. Of course Mr. Fink was usually on his deck waiting. But sometimes he needed to be aroused from a nap. Bolt didn't want to deprive him of the opportunity to yell and scream.

Last year, Mr. Fink had built the fence taller, six or seven feet, a privacy fence he called it. Bolt called it an opportunity. That had been even more fun. Bolt had never pole vaulted, but the thrill of stick-sprinting, grabbing the top of the fence, and swinging up and over it, had convinced him that someday he wanted to try pole vaulting. His legs may be weak, but his arms and shoulders were still strong. And even better, Mr. Fink had gotten more angry, and more determined.

This year Mr. Fink had bought a dog, a Doberman, "Rod," Mr. Fink called him. Bolt wasn't sure whether Mr. Fink had picked the name as a lightning rod, to ground him, or whether the rod was supposed to thrash him. Either way, Bolt renamed the dog "Dobie." Dobie was just one more challenge to get his day started with some excitement. Once he had outrun Dobie and vaulted over the fence, he didn't need any coffee to get his heart pounding.

This morning Mr. Fink was napping on the deck, or pretending to, with Dobie lying beside him. Bolt got up some speed and vaulted over the fence.

"Good morning, Mr. Finklestein," yelled Bolt as he began his sprint. As he suspected, Mr. Fink was already awake and had released Dobie. Bolt turned on the steam and stick-sprinted like his life depended on it. He swung up and over the fence on the Cedar Heights side, his crutches trailing behind him, just as Dobie began nipping at his heels.

One last peek over the fence, a little pixie dust from his wand—after all, this was good magic, he was making a friend—and two doggie treats dropped in front of Dobie. The growl turned into a yelp for more treats.

Bolt was turning to head for breakfast, a smile pulling at the corners of his mouth, when he saw a blur flash in front of him and disappear into the forest. He blinked. That almost looked like Mr. Fink. He glanced back at the deck, just as the same blur shot past him in the opposite direction, and Mr. Fink was still there on the deck. Bolt rubbed his eyes. Wow, that was strange. He needed to eat.

As he stick-hopped to Cedar Heights, he grinned and wondered what obstacle Mr. Fink would come up with next to challenge him. And why did he have that streak in him that loved to aggravate people? Maybe it was brain damage from the lightning. Jerk would agree with that. He smiled and rubbed his hair to lay down the white spike, but it sprang back up.

Half a minute later, Bolt hopped into Cedar Heights. The house—the council house, they called it—was big, full of furniture and people. It was comfortable, not fancy, the kind of place that was a home away from home for him. Many family discussions had taken place around the oval breakfast table. Gramps said the house was called the council house, similar to the Indian council houses. Bolt agreed with that, but he had also heard some strong counsel laid out by Gram and Gramps. He suspected that that Gramps was really spelling it the "counsel" house.

The smell of French toast wafted from the kitchen. He moved past the mantle and pictures of all seven cousins. Gram even had his picture up there, too.

Above Gram's recliner, a single crochet hook floated in mid-air, tugging at a ball of yarn, and creating a stack of doilies. As Bolt passed the kitchen, empty rubber gloves were washing and drying dishes. He smiled and felt for his wand. There was something truly magic about this place.

Bolt found his seat at the big oval table with all four of the five Ohio cousins and both Grandparents.

"We thought you might be sleeping in this morning," said Gram, as she jumped up and planted a kiss on top of Bolt's head. She was as spry as Gramps and appeared to be a few years younger. Always hustling around the kitchen to keep her army fed, her long brown pony tail whipped back and forth. Warm, kind, dark brown eyes seemed to look into his soul. She always knew what he needed. A little shorter than Gramps, her bee-like activity seemed to keep her trim and fit.

"What happened, Master Bolt?" said Regan. "Did that canine monster capture you by the seat of your pants?" She didn't even look up. "I've been working on a transfiguration spell to turn Dobie into a cheetah." She grimaced. "You know how fast those critters can run? We'd be patching your pants every morning. Then you could change your name to Patch."

"Stop it," said Gramps, as he frowned at Regan. "You know magic is only to be used for good."

"What a waste," murmured Regan under her breath.

"Could you repeat that so we could all hear you?" asked Scout, as he grinned at Bolt.

Bolt shook his head. What a crew. He didn't need any brothers with a cousin like Scout. And he sure didn't want any sisters, at least none like Regan. They called her

Rey, probably because of her blond hair. He doubted that it was because of her sunny disposition.

Gram set a plate of French toast in front of him. Bolt was reaching for the syrup when Gram picked up the plate again.

"I forgot to warm them up," she said. "Sorry." She turned around, and Bolt heard her murmur some spell. She continued turning as she put her wand back into her pocket and set the plate back in front of Bolt. "There," said Gram, "that should do it."

The French toast was piping hot. Bolt poured the syrup and dug in.

"Really, Dear," said Gramps, looking at Gram and shaking his head. "Shouldn't we set a better example for the children?"

"What?" said Gram as she hurried off to the kitchen to get some more orange juice.

"Yeah, Gramps," said Lillian. "What's the big deal? If Gram didn't use some magic around here to keep up, she wouldn't be able to take care of all of us, and..." She stopped and put her head down.

Gramps smiled and nodded his head. They called Lillian "Lil," probably because she was so petite, but sometimes she came up with some big doosies.

"Gramps," said Lil, "when are we going to do my passenger rights ceremony?"

"Rite of passage," said Scout, laughing.

"Whatever," said Lil. "I want to get my wand and learn to warm up food like Gram does. Averie was eight when she got hers. I'm eight now."

"So you are, Lil," said Gramps. "We should have a wiener roast tonight and make you an official member of the gang, the Mad River Magic."

"And maybe," said Rey, "Gramps could shorten his sermon on using magic for good down to five minutes instead of thirty." She smiled at Gramps. "I have some important reading to do tonight."

Bolt sat quietly and took it all in, as he shoveled down his second plate of French toast. He loved the chaos of a big family. Hopefully the out-of-state cousins would show up this summer, too. This was home. The girls did get on his nerves at times, but that's why they had a girls' club and the boys had a boys' club. Which reminded him.

When the group left the table, Bolt grabbed Scout. "We need to talk. It's time for a meeting of the boys' club. Meet me at the tree house in fifteen minutes."

Rey looked at them huddling and probably guessed what they were planning. "I think," said Rey, "that it should be the boys' turn to do the dishes." She sneered at Bolt.

Bolt twitched his nose and pointed his wand at Rey. A pair of puke-colored dish-washing gloves appeared on Rey's hands. "There you go," said Bolt, as he chuckled and slapped Rey on the back. Then, imitating Gram's voice, he added, "And don't dawdle, there's lots of other house work to get done."

Bolt and Scout hurried out the back door. A sloppy wet dish rag caught Bolt in the back of the head.

∞ ∞ ∞

Bolt called the boys' club meeting to order. He and Scout looked out the door of the small room to the cable bridge hanging across the Mad River It connected their tree house to the girls' tree house on the other side of the river.

The two tree houses had been Gramps' idea of giving the opposing teams some space, but staying connected with a bridge. Bolt thought the cable bridge was a waste. He couldn't think of any time they had used it. There was a regular bridge just below it, after all. But Gramps was always about reconciliation, as he called it. Whatever.

"I called this meeting," said Bolt, "to discuss the big hole Gramps showed us yesterday." He paused, as his breathing slowed down. "It's really important that we don't breathe a word of this to the girls. Have you said anything about the hole to them?"

Scout shook his head.

"Good," continued Bolt. "Now, I think we need to discuss a way to explore the hole."

"Gramps said to stay away," said Scout, who usually had very little to say. "But I sure would like to get a look down into that thing from directly over the center of the hole. I'd take a laser light, a laser distance measure, and a telescope. There has to be a bottom to it."

"I agree," said Bolt. "But how are we going to get over the top of it? That sounds pretty dangerous to me."

Scout's eyes widened, and he held up a finger. "I have an idea," he said. "When we install the turbo-levitators in the barrel carts, we can fly the carts over the top of the hole."

"Great idea," said Bolt. Why hadn't he thought of that? "Let's get back to the tractor shed and get those turbos finished."

The boys had just climbed down the ramp, when Averie appeared. They called her "Bug," probably because she was always flying from one thing to another. Bolt thought the name was appropriate. She certainly was good at bugging him.

"What are you doing over here?" asked Scout. "Your tree house is on the other side of the river."

"I can go anywhere in this forest I want," said Bug. "I wasn't in your tree house."

"Well, what do you want?" asked Scout, as he watched her suspiciously.

"Gramps wants to talk to you guys," said Bug. "And he said 'Right now!' "

Chapter Four

Flying Barrel Carts

*B*olt and Scout raced through the forest, always game for another opportunity to compete. The trees and foliage insulated the runners from the outside world, like time tubes connecting two different eras. The trails opened up to primitive life at the back of the forest and modern times at the front.

Scout was two years younger than Bolt, and shorter. But with Bolt stick-hopping, it was usually a close race. Today, however, Scout lagged behind. Looking over his shoulder, Bolt couldn't see him. He had probably stopped to talk to the animals or explore a new nook or cranny. He seemed to always have a critter friend and knew what was going on with the animals.

Mind racing faster than his feet, Bolt tried to think of what Gramps could possibly want to talk to them about, unless it was more about the hole. Hopefully there wasn't any bad news. He had heard the occasional rumble coming from the back of the forest this morning. Yeah, it had to be about the hole.

Heart pounding, and panting to catch his breath, Bolt came to an abrupt stop in front of the tractor shed. He kept his eyes down to protect them from the bright light of the welding arc.

"You sure are in a big hurry to get to work," said Gramps, laughing and laying down his welding helmet. "What's the rush?"

"Bug said you wanted to talk to us right away," said Bolt, looking at Gramps with uncertainty.

Gramps scratched his head and smiled. "I think your little cousin has fooled you once again. Where were you and what were you doing when she told you this?"

Bolt paused, beginning to realize what had happened.

"We were back in the forest at the tree house," said Bolt. "We were having a boys' club meeting."

"I see," said Gramps. "And what were you discussing at this meeting?"

Bolt looked down, kicking the gravel with his crutch. That little brat. She was always following them. And now she knew about the hole—or did she?

"I'll be back soon," said Bolt, as he started toward the forest. He'd get to the bottom of this.

"No violence and no threats," Gramps yelled after him. "She's your cousin. And remember, magic is only for good..." His voice trailed off as Bolt stick-sprinted down the trail.

His temper rose hotter and hotter as he bounded faster and faster. Coming around a curve in the trail, he found Scout sitting on a hollow log, feeding a squirrel. It scampered up a tree, and Bolt yelled for Scout to follow him.

When they reached the tree house, Bug was nowhere to be found. But she still had some questions to answer. What had she been up to? They would find out. They sprinted to the hole, but no Bug.

When they returned to the house, no one had seen her. She was obviously hiding. Not a good sign.

Bolt and Scout headed for the tractor shed. Hopefully Gramps had cleared out by now. They needed to get the turbo-levitators finished.

Finding the doors to the shed open, and Gramps and the Kubota gone, they decided that he was probably checking on the hole. It was tempting to follow him, but the prospect of racing the barrel carts through the forest was stronger.

Scout worked his magic, and the first two carts were rigged out and ready to go. The turbo-levitators, or "turbos" as they called them, were tucked under the dashboards. As the boys pulled the carts out of the shed, Bolt noticed that one of the other carts was missing. Maybe Gramps was giving Bug a ride in the forest. That should keep her out of the way. Gramps certainly wouldn't show her the hole.

The boys pulled the carts into the backyard and fired up the turbos. After climbing in and strapping themselves securely, they began to test their new invention. Tentative at first, then speeding up, they flew faster and higher. Scout knew how the turbos worked, but he was always cautious. Bolt was the risk taker. He loved the thrill of power and riding that fine line between control and disaster.

Bolt propelled his cart straight up. Wow, this freedom was awesome. Wouldn't it be fun to fly one of these things over Mr. Fink's yard? But Gramps had always reminded them, "Magic is for good only, and not to be flaunted in the face of unbelievers." Whatever that meant. Old Mr. Fink would certainly believe if he saw this cart buzz Dobie.

Soon the boys were swooping and turning, starting and stopping. The banked turns were clunky, and Scout didn't know how to fix them. But he'd come up with an answer.

Finally they were ready to race the trails through the forest. After agreeing to race the main loop, they lined up on the starting line, and they were off. The carts blasted silently down the trail. The rush of flying through a tunnel put every brain cell on alert. Birds, taken by surprise at the boys' silent appearance, squawked and fluttered out of the way. Scout and Bolt zoomed under branches, dodging back and forth with the curves, as the two remained side by side. Bolt had never experienced anything so exhilarating in his life. This was better than fence vaulting. A flash of red streaked across the trail ahead of him. It must have been a cardinal.

When they reached the back corners of the trail, Scout slowed to negotiate the first curve, but Bolt sped ahead. Sliding to the outside of the curve, he missed a tree by inches. Then a low hanging branch caught him and took him down. Scout stopped to check for damages. Bolt's cart was scratched, but he wasn't hurt. They checked to be certain that everything was working, refastened his crutches to the outside of the barrel, and the race resumed.

As they reached the end of the back stretch and the final big curve, Bolt saw another streak of red in his peripheral vision. Turning, he discovered Bug pulling up beside him in a barrel cart. What! Where did she get that cart? Gramps! This was supposed to be their secret.

"What are you doing?" Bolt shouted at her.

"I'll race you to the finish line," she yelled back. Aviator goggles covered her eyes, and a white scarf wrapped around her neck, streaming behind her.

Bolt clenched his teeth. He'd show her.

They hit the final series of turns before the home stretch. Bolt slowed to negotiate the trees. Bug shot ahead. She was going to crash. That'll teach her.

But she didn't. She wove in and out of the tight turns at twice the speed of Bolt and Scout, then blasted out of the final turn and raced to the finish line a full one hundred yards ahead of the boys.

As Bolt flew across the finish line, pounding his fist on his cart in rage, Bug performed vertical figure-eights and barrel rolls in the sky above him.

He got out of his cart and turned off the turbo. Gramps stood in the grassy opening, grinning and looking up at Bug's aerobatics. Bolt slammed his crutches into the ground with each hop toward Gramps, but Gramps kept his eyes on Bug, ignoring Bolt.

What was going on here? Bolt could feel the anger coming to a boil under his red hair and flushed face. First Gramps had been amused that Bug had spied on them. Now he had stolen one of their turbos and installed it in a cart for her. He hadn't even asked. Man, he wasn't supposed to know about the turbos. Bolt had never confronted Gramps before, but...maybe he wasn't really one of the grandkids after all.

Scout stepped up beside him. "How could you, Gramps?" He stomped his foot. "We helped you build the carts, and we invented the turbos. This was *our* project."

"Was it?" asked Gramps as he continued watching Bug. "Where did you get the ideas for the turbos?"

"I found them," said Scout, starting to hesitate.

"And where did you find those ideas?" continued Gramps, still grinning.

Bolt knew that the ideas had come from Gramps' old magic books, including notes written in the margins.

Scout didn't answer.

"Did you boys ask me if you could use those ideas?" said Gramps. "Why didn't you say anything when we were working on the carts?"

Bolt and Scout hung their heads.

"And for the record," said Gramps, "Bug helped me build her cart. She wanted it to be a surprise."

Bug pulled out of a dive and came to a soft landing in front of them.

Scout ran up to her cart and looked at Gramps, seeming to forget his anger. "How did you make those turns so tight?" he asked. He seemed more curious than angry.

"Look under the dash board," said Gramps, as he approached the cart.

Scout practically dragged Bug out of her cart so he could look. He ducked under the dash, then pulled his head out with a big grin. "Two turbos!" he said. "How did you discover that you needed two?"

"Do you remember the book where you found the ideas for the turbos?" asked Gramps. "And did you notice that one of the pages had been torn out?"

"Oh, yeah," said Scout as he slapped his palm to his forehead. "It never dawned on me..."

"Why didn't you tell us, Gramps?" asked Bolt.

"You didn't ask," said Gramps. "See what happens when we selfishly keep secrets instead of sharing knowledge."

Bolt's temper was calming, but he still didn't like the idea of having no secrets. That was the idea of the boys' club. "You're not saying that we boys can't go off and do anything without telling the girls?" he said. That would be really stupid.

"No," said Gramps. He chuckled. "You all have different interests. I'll bet Rey and Lil are holed up in the attic, right now, with their stash of magic books, learning new spells to use on you guys. I just hope that you can all learn to work together. Someday your life may depend on it."

Scout was already pulling his cart into the tractor shed to install a second turbo. Bolt followed him with his cart.

He thought over the events of the day thus far. He couldn't imagine ever working with the girls, especially Rey. Some things were just not possible.

Chapter Five

Rite of Passage

The time for Lil's rite of passage ceremony had finally arrived. It would be a picnic supper at the pond, with all of Gram's magical fixings. Even though it wasn't about him, Bolt could hardly wait. His stomach growled as if he hadn't already eaten two meals that day. The smell of Gram's fried chicken drew him into the kitchen. But every time he tried to sneak a piece of cheese from the relish tray, Rey snapped him with a wet dish towel.

"You two, get out of the kitchen," said Gram with frustration in her voice. "If you're going to fight, take it outside. I can't work when you're in the way."

"You want to duel?" said Rey, pointing her wand at Bolt. "Winner gets to throw the loser into the pond."

"You're on," said Bolt, whipping out his wand and lifting a crutch as if it were a shield in a sword fight.

Gram stepped between the two combatants, rubbing her hands on her apron. "Bolt, will you drive the Tiger to the back door?" she said. "And Rey, help Lil get everything covered and ready for the ride to the pond."

Bolt tossed an olive at Rey's backside as he headed out the door. She certainly deserved all the grief he could give her. He remembered how, at her rite of passage ceremony, and right after Gramps had discussed the importance of using magic only for good, she had immediately given all the boys a poison ivy rash.

And before that, Bolt remembered his ceremony from four years ago. He had been the first to get one of Gramps' magic wands. He rubbed the pencil-sized oak and cedar instrument, feeling a sense of power, reliving that special moment. He wasn't sure his legs had become stronger, but they didn't seem to be getting weaker anymore, although he knew that the odds were against him, and the weakness would eventually spread to his upper body. He definitely had found new courage to take on any obstacle that got in his way. Yeah, it was the first time he had really felt like he belonged. His mom had always tried to make a home for him. But with her work and never being home, and Jerk taking over the house, Cedar Heights had become his second home, or really, his first. And the rite of passage ceremony had made it official. Now, tonight would be Lil's turn.

Bolt drove the Tiger to the back door and got out of the way. Rey held the doors open. Gram stood at the back of the Tiger. Pointing her wand at the kitchen, she commanded, "*Metemyilo!*" Light burst from her wand and streamed to the kitchen. An invisible band struck up a military marching song, and the supper dishes paraded out of the house, then packed themselves into the Tiger. Lil yelled with delight, marching below the floating food.

The whole family cheered, except Gramps. Shaking his head, he climbed into the Tiger beside Gram. The cousins hopped into the carts, and the barrel cart train headed down the path to the pond at the back of the forest. Bolt felt contentment, except for an empty stomach. He looked to the left, toward the corner of the forest where the hole was. What were they going to do about that?

Ten minutes later they pulled into a large grassy meadow that sloped away from them to the far end, where the Mad River gurgled over stones and gravel on its way south to join the Great Miami River. Gramps called the river and the grandchildren Mad River Magic, and Bolt was certain that he'd hear, once again, about the magical properties of its water and the story behind the magic.

Nestled into a small inlet off the river was the quiet water they called their magic pond. A covered pavilion stood beside the pond. A wooden deck held two picnic tables, enough for the whole gang. Gramps pulled the barrel-cart train up to the edge of the pavilion, and the crew scrambled out.

While Gram once again performed her "*metemyilo*" spell, Scout and Bug detached two of the carts with turbos. They hopped in and lifted off, and within seconds were racing over the pond and dive-bombing the pavilion.

Bolt leaned on his crutches, watching and laughing. When Scout buzzed Rey, she screamed and shook her fist at him. Gramps shook his head with disapproval. Lil had not seen the carts fly before and watched in amazement.

Finally Gramps pointed his wand at them. "Get down here," he yelled, "or I'll crash both of you into the pond."

The group gathered for supper, talking excitedly about the turbo carts.

"Gramps," asked Rey, "have you made a turbo for me?"

"I want one, too," said Lil. She scowled at Scout, aiming an invisible wand at him, as if she were ready to challenge him to an aerial dogfight.

---

[1] Follow the path! (may-taym-yee-lo)

19

"You'll all get one," said Gramps. "But I need to give you girls lessons, or you'll be crashing into trees."

"Are you implying that girls can't fly as well as boys?" said Rey.

"No," said Gramps. "The boys had some near misses with trees before they were ready to be turned loose."

Bolt kept his head down, emptying his plate as fast as he could shovel in the food. Why was Gramps taking away all the boys' fun? The turbos were their plan, even if Gramps had invented them. He and Scout didn't go invading the girls' magic library. But come to think of it, maybe he should. He just might learn some spells to better investigate the hole in the back of the forest.

Supper ended, and everyone helped Gram load the dishes into the Tiger. Shiny yellow table cloths glittered with the reflection of the setting sun and converted the rough picnic tables into magical stands. Candles flickered in brass candelabras as the evening grew darker.

A pencil-sized wand of white oak and red cedar lay on a purple velvet cloth on a pedestal stand between the tables. Sitting in front of the wand, Lil rested her arms on both sides of the velvet cloth, guarding and admiring her soon-to-be personal magic wand.

When everyone was seated on the picnic benches, Gramps appeared out of the shadows, carrying a glass pitcher of water from the Mad River. Glowing in the dark, the water revealed that Gramps had added his magic phosphorescent powder.

Bolt grinned, thinking of the first time he had gone for a night-time swim in the pond. When the water had gradually begun to glow, he had jumped out, and the cousins had laughed at him. Then he'd seen Gramps sprinkling the magic powder into the pond. It was now one of the cousins' favorite summertime activities, moonlight swims in the glowing Mad River Magic.

Gramps set the pitcher of water on the candle-lit table and dropped the wand into the water. The red tip began to glow. Then, stepping back, he took Lil's hand and led her to the edge of the pavilion. Behind them the setting sun reflected off the surface of the pond, casting a golden red glow. Bolt had to admit, it was an unbelievably beautiful setting.

Gramps cleared his throat to begin.

"How about the five-minute version tonight?" said Rey, as she drummed her fingers impatiently on the table.

Gramps smiled at her. "Maybe, if you hear the story one more time, you'll begin to understand what I'm trying to tell you."

She rolled her eyes.

Bolt aimed his wand at her, as if lecturing her.

She stuck out her tongue.

"A long time ago," said Gramps, "an elderly wizard moved to this forest to escape the persecution of a world that didn't understand magic. The rest of the world thought that magic was evil and dark. And wizards who were caught in those days were often tortured or even killed.

"Now, this wizard," continued Gramps, "was a good wizard. He only did magic to help people and to make his world a better place. His power came from beyond him, and it flowed through him to do all kinds of wonderful things. When the wizard moved to the forest, there were still Indians living in the Mad River valley. The wizard was accepted by the Indians and spent many days with them, learning from their medicine men and religious leaders. He freely shared his knowledge with them, and they all benefited.

"As his knowledge and power increased, his reputation with the wildlife became known far and wide. Birds with broken wings appeared at his door, and he healed them. Rabbits with infected feet limped to his house, and he helped them as well.

"Although the animals knew him, the settlers and English community didn't know his secret. To them, he looked just like everyone else. But one day, while a carpenter was helping him build a new barn, the carpenter fell and broke his leg. Well, the wizard felt sorry for him, because the carpenter would be unable to work for many weeks. So the wizard held the crooked bones in his hands, and looking up into the sky, he said '*Kiikilo!*[2]'

"The leg began to move, the bones straightened, the gash where the bones had protruded closed. The carpenter looked at the wizard with amazement, stood, and walked.

"The wizard asked the carpenter to tell no one. But of course that didn't happen. So the wizard had to isolate himself even deeper within the forest."

Gramps went on and on with his story, explaining that the old wizard had passed down his books and his magic to his son and his grandson. And when the grandson was a very old man, Gramps had met him and expressed interest in buying the forest. After spending time with the old wizard and convincing him of a real interest in his magic, Gramps had been allowed to buy the forest. He renamed it Cedar Heights.

By now, Rey was beginning to nod off. But Lil listened intently as if she had never heard the story before.

As Gramps finished his tale, he described the special properties of the white oak lumber that had been harvested from the old wizard's forest, and how it had been used to build covered bridges, barns, barrels, and even sail boats. He told how the wood had survived centuries.

---

[2] Heal! (keee-kee-lo)

More interesting, though, was the power the wizard attributed to the water of the Mad River. The wizard had discovered a powder that, when mixed with the water from the river, caused the water to glow. He had made all his potions from this mixture, and guarded the formula very carefully. Gramps claimed that when the old wizard died, he had been buried at the headwaters of the Mad River, and had taken a large bag of the powder to his grave with him.

And finally, when Gramps purchased the Cedar Heights forest, he had cleaned out some old barns and discovered a large cache of magic books. One of the books had been a diary. Gramps had found the formula for the potions, and even more important was the fact that he had found some clues to the source of the powder. He also found references to a bright red light in a discussion of the magic water and the heart of a red cedar log.

At this point Gramps refused to answer questions as to where his powder came from, but claimed his was the very same powder the wizard had used.

Rey was asleep, her head resting on the table. Everyone else was smiling and waiting anxiously for the culmination of Lil's ceremony.

Gramps carried the pitcher of glowing water to Lil, pulled the wand out of the water, and tapped Lil on the head three times. "*Manetoowiiyilo!*[3]" said Gramps.

Suddenly a circle of light perched on Lil's head, like a radiant crown with tiny flames of fire. Gramps handed Lil her new wand and gave her a big hug.

The wand began to reshape. It stretched into a delicate form that reflected Lil. Bolt pulled his wand from his pocket and ran his fingers over it, remembering how his wand had grown at his rite-of-passage ceremony. The lower end of the wand had thickened into two stems, side by side, as if they were two strong legs. Bolt smiled and tapped his wand. It slid back into a shorter and smaller form, camouflaged as a pencil. He slid it back into his pocket.

"And now," announced Gramps, "you may light the bulbs."

Lil smiled and pronounced, "*Wa'the'kilo!*[4]" Light erupted from the glowing red tip of her wand. She held it to her mouth and blew. A stream of sparks flew to the light bulbs, and instantly the pavilion was flooded in light. Rey woke up from her nap and joined the family as they cheered, then formed a ring around Lil to participate in the final part of the ceremony.

Gram stepped into the center beside Lil, holding a s'more pouch. She gave Lil a big hug. "You are now officially a member of Mad River Magic," announced Gram. "But, to be fully protected, you will need more than the wand. You will also need food and defenses for any journey you might take."

---

[3] Take power! (mah-nay-too-weee-yee-lo)

[4] Let there be light! (wah-thay-kee-lo)

Gram placed the crocheted pack into Lil's outstretched hands.

"This s'more pack will provide a never-ending supply of goodies," said Gram. "You simply hold the pack to your heart and think of what you would like to eat. Would you now magibake your first meal, Lil?"

Beaming with delight, Lil clutched the pack to her chest. She swayed back and forth, licking her lips. Bolt remembered his first magibake meal at his ceremony. He had seen "power" bars advertised on TV. Oh, how he had wished for stronger legs. When the power bars magically appeared in his s'more pack, he had eaten all the extra bars that first night. At his next doctor's visit, doc had told him that he was surprised the Becker's muscular dystrophy had not progressed or moved to his upper body. Bolt wasn't surprised. He knew why, and he gave his legs and crutches a progressively harder workout.

When he repeatedly broke his crutches, the doctors had replaced his wooden crutches with metal ones. He remembered them saying, "Just like you, Bolt, these crutches will bend, but they won't break."

Bolt's attention returned to Lil's ceremony.

"Now you may serve your first magical meal," said Gram.

Lil moved around the circle as each member reached in and pulled out a chocolate chip cookie. When everyone had their cookie, they raised it in a cheer. "To Lil!"

"Now," said Gram, "would you see what else is in the pack?"

Lil pulled out a stack of small starched doilies.

"Those are defense disks," said Gram.

"I would be happy to demonstrate," said Bolt, pointing at Rey who stood on the opposite side of the circle.

The group chuckled.

"You may demonstrate," said Gram, "but not on Rey." She pointed at a post ten feet from the pavilion. "Use that."

Bolt took a disk and spun it like a Frisbee. Just before impact, the disk blossomed into a net and wrapped itself tightly around the post. Lil jumped and cheered.

Gram gave Lil another big hug and kissed her on top of her head. "Welcome to Mad River Magic," said Gram. "You may be the youngest, but you will be mighty." Tears ran down Gram's cheeks.

Bolt didn't know why, but tears formed in his eyes, too. It happened with each ceremony. He couldn't prevent it. Yes, this was his family. He quickly wiped his eyes.

It was late, and the family loaded up the last few things for the drive back to the house. Everyone had climbed into a barrel cart or the Tiger, when a strange noise began coming from the pond. Gramps had the Tiger's lights on and pulled around so the headlights pointed down toward the pond.

Bubbles broke the surface of the pond, making loud pops. Then suddenly the pond dropped about twelve inches.

Bolt looked at Gramps. He was trying to remain calm.

"Let's head back to the house," said Gramps, his jaws clenching and relaxing, and his hands tightly squeezing the steering wheel.

Bolt swallowed hard. He didn't have a clue as to what was going on with that big growing hole in the back of the forest, but he bet that it had something to do with the pond. And someone better do something to fix it...before it was too late.

Chapter Six

Ring of Fire

*B*olt looked around the library. Shelves filled with old books lined all the walls, giving the room the smell of musty paper. Man, this place was huge. He'd only been in here once before, looking for Gramps, and hadn't paid much attention. He should've asked questions then. Now he was going to have to wing it. So where did Gramps keep those old magic books the girls were studying?

Gramps was giving the girls barrel cart flying lessons today. Bug was probably showing off while Rey and Lil were learning the basics. Well, that was just fine. Bolt didn't want Rey to know he was here. Okay, let's find the books. They had to be here somewhere.

Wow, there were lots of Indian artifacts in here. He stopped at a display case and studied the arrow heads, spear tips, and club heads. Man, those things could do some serious damage. Did Gramps find these things in the Cedar Heights forest? He needed to ask Gramps where he could look.

And the pictures on the walls, he hadn't noticed them before. As he moved around the room and studied the pictures, he could see that Gramps was into this Indian stuff, big time. One picture displayed an Indian village on a hill overlooking a river. Was that the Mad River? A second picture showed a proud chief wearing a blue coat. The title at the bottom of the picture was "Chief Blue Jacket." A third picture was tucked back into a corner, and it really drew Bolt in. A huge fire in the center of a village was surrounded by a dance ring. Indians of all ages were dancing in a circle that had to be over forty feet in diameter. Wow, there was something that made Bolt want to climb right into that picture and look around.

He shook his head. Focusing more closely on the books, he moved around the room exploring the shelves in the dim light. He'd caught Rey talking to Lil about the secret access to the magic books, something about a hidden staircase. And Gramps had talked about the attic. There didn't seem to be any break in the woodwork that would lend itself to a hidden door. He stepped back into the middle of the room and rubbed his chin. What was he missing?

Aha! A faint line appeared in the wall above and below the picture of the dance ring. Could that be the secret access? Was the secret library in the attic? He began looking for a switch. Nothing. He'd heard Rey talking to herself in here. Was there a magic word? Leave it to Gramps to make it complicated.

Bolt rubbed his hair, then pointed his wand at the picture. "Hidden staircase." Nothing. "Steps." Nothing "Magic books." Still nothing. He looked behind the picture. Nothing there, either.

Hey, Gram's magic commands were always in a strange language. And Gramps talked about the wizard and his Indian connections. Were those spells in an Indian language? He scanned the shelves. Yup, an old book pulled out a bit—a Shawnee dictionary—Say *it in Shawnee!*. Now he was getting somewhere. He grabbed the book. Yes, a dog-eared page. He opened it. Half way down the right side was a finger-smudged entry. "dance ring—weewaaweyaayaaki."

Bolt pointed his wand at the picture. "*Weewaaweyaayaaki![5]*"

The picture disappeared in a cloud of smoke, and that burst into a ring of fire. Bolt jumped back and was about to run for a fire extinguisher, when he noticed the fire was consuming nothing. And behind the ring had appeared a staircase. Wow, this was becoming fun. No wonder Rey was addicted to these books. He vaulted through the ring and hopped up the steps to total darkness.

"*Wa'the'kilo!*" He knew that one. The room magically filled with light. And there weren't any light bulbs. He stick-hopped back down the staircase and snatched the dictionary. He was going to have to get himself a pocket version. That old fox, Gramps. He was always giving Gram a rough time for using her spells. And look what he had been up to.

Back in the secret library, Bolt looked around. This was a tight space, brightly illuminated, but hot and stuffy. He had to stoop on one side where the ceiling was low, following the roof line above. These books looked ancient. They filled about half the shelves of the ten foot by ten foot space.

He scanned the shelves, afraid to touch anything lest it fall apart. What was he looking for anyway? He and Scout needed a way to safely explore the aperture, or better yet, to seal it off forever. But how? If Gramps didn't know, there wasn't much chance he'd find something.

---

[5] Dance ring (waay-waah-wee-yaah-yaah-kee)

A stack of books sat on the floor in the corner, probably books Rey and Lil were studying. He picked up the top one, *Spells and Curses for Personal Protection.* Now this looked promising. Opening the front cover, he glanced at the table of contents. "Spells for Beginners." That would be him. He opened to the section. Hey, someone had already been here. Underlined words filled the yellow page, and a few pages were even dog-eared. Come on, girls, show a little respect. He wondered if Gramps had seen that.

Sitting on the narrow floor with his legs stretched out in front of him, he began studying. Funny how this had never interested him before, but now he was totally caught up in the quaint old language. He heard footsteps in the library below. Blast. Who was that? He was trapped. Looking around again, he found no place to hide.

"Lil, is that you up there?" It was Rey.

How was he going to explain this? She couldn't learn about the aperture. Quick! He flipped open the dictionary. "Hurry. Quick!–*Wipi!*" Yes.

Bolt lifted the magic book and placed his wand between the book and his temple. "*Wipi!*" He felt a quick zap on his temple, then placed the book back on the corner pile.

Rey stopped at the top of the staircase. "What are you doing up here?"

He couldn't let her know. Stay cool, man. "Oh, just checking out these old magic books," said Bolt. Divert her attention. "You found any good spells for flying?" He laughed.

"How did you get up here?" demanded Rey. "Gramps said Lil and I were the only ones who knew the password."

"Password?" said Bolt. The old rascal. First it was the barrel carts, and now the secret library. "What password?"

"To get up here," said Rey. "Where did you..." She glanced at the dictionary. "Give me that."

"Does this belong to you?" said Bolt, holding the dictionary behind his back. "I recall Gramps talking about sharing information. You don't seem to be interested in sharing."

"What are you doing up here anyway?" asked Rey. "You've never been interested in magic spells before. This should be the girls' space." She put her hands on her hips and glared at him. "What are you really looking for?"

"Nothing," said Bolt, laughing. He pushed past her and hopped down the steps. "Just wanted to see what was keeping you and Lil so occupied." He put the dictionary back in its spot. After tapping the dictionary with his wand, he tapped his temple, "*Wipi!*" He felt another zap and hurried out the door.

Great, now Rey would be even more paranoid. He should've had Scout keep guard for him. At least now he knew how to get in.

He wondered if the secret staircase would close with someone in the attic. *"Wiiwaawiyaayaaki!"*

Chapter Seven

Swallowed Alive

olt and Scout zipped around the Cedar Heights trails in their barrel carts, like jets blasting through a tunnel. They were racing for the aperture, and they wanted to get there before Rey and her female posse started looking for them. When they had left the house, Lil and Rey were circling the tractor shed in their carts, moving slowly, while Bug did stunts above them. It looked like they needed a lot of practice. He and Scout shouldn't have to worry about them today, but you never knew. Rey wasn't going to take his answer for an answer. She would come snooping, looking to see what he was up to. Why did she think she needed to know everything? And what had Bug told her?

Shafts of light piercing the woodland canopy created a hypnotic strobe effect, once again giving the illusion of traveling back in time, as they raced for the back of the forest. Bolt was jarred from his thoughts when Scout passed him, his thumb held up with satisfaction. Yeah, these barrel carts handled much better with two turbos installed. He wondered how quickly Rey and Lil would learn to fly. Then there would be no privacy.

Bolt and Scout reached the aperture and were standing outside the fence, when a flock of noisy crows tried to land on the shiny Hemlock. The ground shook and a low rumble announced that the birds were about to be punished for daring to trespass. The translucent camera aperture appeared in mid-air beside the black and white tree. It opened, and a dusty puff accompanied the disappearance of the birds, before the aperture closed and disappeared, and the birds were no more.

"Did you see that?" asked Scout, his eyes wide with amazement.

"Do you think we can fly over that thing?" said Bolt.

Scout looked at him in disbelief. "I think we should fly around it. I don't want to get over the top of that tree or anywhere near it."

"Let's do it," said Bolt. He hopped into his barrel cart and strapped his crutches in place.

Scout hesitated.

"Are you coming?" asked Bolt.

"I don't know, man," said Scout, frozen halfway in his cart.

"C'mon," said Bolt, and he lifted off.

Scout slowly lowered himself into his seat and followed Bolt. They began circling the large depression in the ground below them, at first from a hundred feet up. Then, as he gained confidence, Bolt dropped down closer and closer to the tree. Scout kept his distance.

From this vantage point Bolt didn't see anything particularly alarming. Should he zip past the tree for a closer look? He was contemplating such a move when he saw movement out of the corner of his eye. What was that? He turned his head to see Rey, Lil, and Bug appear at the fence, each flying their own cart. Blast!

Bolt flew to the fence, followed by Scout.

"What are you girls doing back here?" demanded Bolt. Why did Gramps have to give the girls everything? They should be back at the house or in the library.

"What's that?" asked Rey, pointing to the tree in the middle of the great hole.

"You girls aren't supposed to be back here," said Scout.

"Oh, yeah, then why are you back here?" answered Bug.

"This is dangerous," said Bolt, in a voice of great concern. "You girls should go back to the house."

"I'm not going anywhere until you explain what's going on here," said Rey. "Is this why you were in the magic library? What were you looking for?"

"Look, you girls aren't supposed to know about this," said Bolt. "If you go back to the house now, I won't tell Gramps that you were here." On the other hand, maybe if he told Gramps, he would ground the girls. Yeah, he'd probably ground all of them.

"Right," said Rey. "I believe that as much as I believed your answer in the magic library."

"Yeah," said Bug. "You can't make me do anything." She hopped into her barrel cart and lifted off.

"Wait!" yelled Bolt, as he tried to catch up with her and steer her away from the hole. Blast, the girls were always messing up something.

Before he knew what was happening, the girls were following Bug. Then Scout joined in the chase. Now the whole gang was circling the big hole. Bolt was trying to stay between Bug and the hemlock. Everyone was yelling. No one was listening. Someone was going to get hurt.

Then, suddenly, the low rumble began to rise from deep within the earth. Bolt glanced down and saw that the ground was shaking. The aperture materialized beside the hemlock, and in that instant, Bug dived below him and made a bee line for the tree.

Bolt dove to the left, trying to cut her off, but she was too fast. She was going to fly right over the top of the hemlock. His gut tightened. He almost pulled out of his dive. This was going to end badly. But he stayed on her tail.

"Bug, stop!" yelled Bolt. "Stay away from that tree."

She kept going, even picking up speed, pumping her fist in the air.

He turned to check on the rest of the gang and was horrified to see that they were all following. "No!" He screamed. "Get back."

But they kept following. Even Scout.

His hands were suddenly sweaty. His heart was racing. This couldn't be real.

Bug was over the top of the hemlock now and was instantly pulled into a tight spin. Bolt felt his cart lose control, and then his cart followed hers. As he spun horizontally, he saw flashes of the basin around him. Then, the aperture in front of him opened like a giant mouth that was ready to swallow them.

Bug was screaming.

Glimpses of the yelling gang behind him spun by. Scout's eyes were wide, his mouth open, but silent.

"Bug, no!" yelled Lil.

And then they entered the aperture through a cloud of gray dust. The aperture closed, and absolute darkness engulfed them.

Silence instantly snuffed out all sound. Bolt felt his body expanding, then immediately slammed with a force that crushed him from all sides, taking away his ability to breathe. His body began spinning like a bullet fired from a rifle, and he was blasting through space. No light. No sound. He was going to die.

Chapter Eight

Slippery Glass Trap

The compressive force began to lift, and Bolt could breathe again. Complete darkness surrounded him. Lifting his hand in front of his face, he saw nothing. Total silence gave him the eerie feeling that maybe he was already dead. A cold shiver ran through his body. He tried to yell, but couldn't even hear his voice in his head.

What was happening? His breath was coming quickly. Other than the chill, he felt nothing. He dared not hold his arm out of the barrel cart for fear that he was blasting through a tunnel. At least he was still in his cart. Straining to see or hear anything, he searched for evidence of the rest of the gang, but found nothing.

Touching his shirt pocket, he felt his wand. Would it work? He held it in front of him. *"Wa'the'kilo!"* There was no sound of his voice, but the space inside the barrel cart lit up. He let out a deep sigh. What was this place?

Why could his wand's light not penetrate the darkness around him? And why didn't he see the light from anyone else's wand? He thought frantically. At least some of the gang should be screaming. This wasn't possible. He had never heard or read of anything like this before. Was he dreaming? This must be a fantasy movie.

His face was wet with sweat, his shirt soaked. He would not cry. Remembering Gram and Gramps praying at meals, Bolt whispered, "I don't know if you're out there God, or can even hear me. But please help me...and the rest of the gang."

A whistling noise, like a decelerating jet engine, began faintly and grew louder. A breeze hit him in the face and dried his sweat. The temperature became warmer. He gulped. This didn't feel like falling. In fact, even though he hadn't felt like he was moving, now he seemed to be slowing down. A faint gray circle appeared ahead of him, and then he saw flashes of light and dark alternating as he blasted past them.

The circle became larger and lighter, and the bands of light and dark slowed. Soon dots appeared ahead of him. Were they the carts of the rest of the gang? Behind him he saw more dots. He tried yelling again. Now he could hear his voice in his head, but the sound was muffled.

Within seconds the circle of gray became huge. Bolt definitely saw the rest of the gang, with everyone still in their carts, their screaming becoming louder and louder. And in the next instant he felt a jarring deceleration and bumped to a stop.

Where was this place? He touched his arms and face. They felt normal. Looking around, the light was dim, as if they were in a fog. He climbed out of his barrel cart and promptly slipped and fell. What was he standing on? It was as slippery as a mossy rock in the Mad River. Oh, he wished he were there right now.

The girls were screaming. They were certainly all present. There was no doubt about that.

Hanging onto the barrel cart, Bolt pulled himself up and grabbed his crutches. Scout sat silently in his cart, eyes wide.

"Hey, girls," yelled Bolt. "Stop screaming. We're all here. Is everyone okay?"

"Where are we?" asked Rey.

The rest of the gang was climbing out of their carts, chattering loudly. Well, not Scout.

"Be careful," said Bolt. "The floor is slippery."

Everyone managed to discover that for themselves. They just wouldn't listen. In fact, they were all talking at once. At least no one was hurt.

Bolt looked around again. Even though the light was dim, it didn't appear to be coming from any particular direction or any particular source. There were no colors, everything was a shade of gray. And he couldn't see any distinct objects, other than the gang. Where were they?

He knelt to feel the slippery floor. Strange. Slippery, but dry. There seemed to be a coating of something on the floor. He lifted his hand to his face and blew. A gray dust rose in front of him. He wasn't about to taste it.

Taking a deep breath, he smelled nothing. At least there must be oxygen. "Hello!" he yelled, listening for an echo. But all he heard was the chatter of Rey and Bug and Lil. Funny, he felt like he was in a large enclosed area. Why no echo?

By now Scout was beside him. "Where are we?" asked Scout, in a quiet and tentative voice.

"I wish I knew," said Bolt. "I've never heard of anything like this. It doesn't feel cold like a cavern. I can't tell where the light is coming from. The ground is dry, but slippery. Man, this is weird."

"How are we going to get back?" asked Scout.

Bolt didn't want to answer. "Let's explore this space," he said. "You girls stay close to your carts so you don't get lost. Let's stay together."

Turning to Scout, Bolt said, "I'm going to move away from the carts. You stay here, so I can find my way back."

"Don't go too far," said Scout.

Bolt wished he had someone older to turn to. Oh, if this were only a dream. He pinched himself again. No such luck.

He moved away from the carts, sliding his feet and crutches like he was skating on ice, turning frequently to make certain he could still see the rest of the gang. About thirty feet out, his outstretched hand met a wall that slanted away from him. This felt slippery, just like the floor. It extended as high as he could reach, and he couldn't see the top, either. Squatting carefully to keep from falling, he felt the wall until it met the floor. It made a curved transition. This was like being in a bowl. He began to move to his right, and indeed the wall curved smoothly until he found himself on the other side of the gang.

He made his way back to Scout. "I think we're in a big sixty foot bowl," he said. "And I can't reach the top of it. Let's see if we can move one of the carts over to the wall and stand on it."

"It's a trap," said Rey.

Lil began to cry. "I want to go back to Gram and Gramps. I want my mom and dad."

"Let's see if we can fly our carts," said Bug. She climbed back into her cart. "Come on. Lift off."

The cart lifted off the floor a few feet, but wouldn't go any higher.

"It feels like it wants to fly," said Bug, "but it just won't move, like it's tied down."

As they were pushing Bolt's cart to the wall, a beam of light shone above them, piercing the fog or dust, or whatever it was. It was thirty feet up, and as it got brighter, it turned into two beams.

"Shh," said Bolt. "Quiet."

The group froze. They heard two doors slam shut. Voices approached.

"Why do these alarms always come in during the light hours?" said a low grumpy voice.

"Hey, this one was a big one," answered a high-pitched whiny male voice. "I don't think this is any false alarm."

Suddenly a bright gray light was shining in the gang's faces.

"See," said Whiny voice, "we caught five."

"That should make the boss happy," said Grumpy voice. "Turn on the hoist. Let's see what we have."

Rey gasped. Bolt put his hand over her mouth.

She tore it away. "What difference does it make?" she said. "They already know we're down here."

"Everyone, get in your cart," yelled Bolt. "When they lift you up, as soon as you clear the top, try to fly again."

Bolt felt ropes emerging from the floor as he jumped into his cart. Then his cart was lifted up, along with the rest of the gang.

"Quick," yelled Bolt, "turn on your turbos."

As the large net raised the gang above the top of the bowl, Bolt made his move. The cart sprang forward. Yes, it worked. But he was surrounded by a net that reached high above him and converged in a lift point. The rest of the gang began zipping around the net. But they were trapped. There was no escape.

Their captors began laughing. "Look," said Whiny. "They're bouncing around like bees."

"What are those strange contraptions they're flying in?" asked Grumpy. "Should we introduce them to our flying truck?"

Two burly men in gray stood below them, holding their sides as they laughed. Beside the men, floating on air, sat a dark gray vehicle with a cab in the front like a truck, and a huge empty cage in the back. The vehicle rested a few inches above the ground, but displayed no visible wheels. And the vehicle was silent.

One of the men threw a switch. The net swung around beside the truck, then began to lower the gang to the floor.

Chapter Nine

Welcome to the Strata

The net hit the floor with a thud. Bolt and the rest of the gang froze. Grumpy and Whiny were close enough now for a better look, and their appearance made Bolt speechless.

Both men, if that's what you called them, were...well, fuzzy. They were proportioned like humans. Their faces were shaped like humans', but their features looked translucent, as if you could see right through them. It reminded Bolt of the holographic aperture back at that strange tree. Was this real? He looked around, but saw nothing except gray and the translucent people.

These two were dressed totally in dark gray, almost black. Their uniforms looked like normal coveralls, but seamless and with a zipper in the front. Their faces—Bolt couldn't stop staring—their eyes were dark and piercing, floating in faces that looked like a hazy dust cloud. Weird. Dark gray hair poked out from under simple military-style caps. And on the front of the cap was a logo, a black apple.

"What are ya looking at kid?" said Grumpy, glaring at Bolt. "You never seen a stratoid before?"

"Nu-nu-nothing," stammered Bolt. "Where are we?"

"We'll ask the questions," said Grumpy. "Where you from?"

"Let us out of this net immediately," demanded Rey. Bolt heard the fear in her voice, although she was doing a good job of hiding it. "What are you doing with us?"

"Like I said," answered Grumpy, "we'll ask the questions. Now shut up. Turning to the whiny-voiced stratoid, he said, "Noctus, get up on top of the cage. Let's load them up. Pull them out one at a time, and don't let them get away. This group looks like runners. And pitch those funny toys they're riding. There's no room for them in the slammer."

"Got it, Subter," answered Noctus. He climbed up on top of the cage. "Bring 'em up."

"What is this place?" asked Bolt. "And where are you taking us?"

"Welcome to the Strata," said grumpy-voiced Subter. "We're taking you to Extor. He's the boss around here. Now shut up and let us do our job."

The net and carts banged on top of the cage. Noctus reached for an unnoticed opening. Bolt moved closer. Hey, why hadn't he seen that? When Noctus reached inside to grab a gang member, Bolt was ready.

"Come on," yelled Bolt. He flew his cart right at Noctus' chest, throwing him backwards on top of the cage. He put his cart down on top of him, immobilizing him while the rest of the gang zipped through the opening and hovered over the truck.

"Bug," yelled Bolt, "knock over Subter."

"Yeah," yelled Bug, pointing at Subter as she charged him. She came in low, then pulled up under his chin, like an uppercut. Subter fell backwards, where Bug sat her cart on top of him. "How's that?"

"Good job, Bug," said Bolt. "Now Scout, see if you can work those controls and set the net back down on the ground level."

Scout zoomed to the control panel next to the edge of the bowl. His cart spun out as the wheels hit the slippery dust. Eagerly inspecting the unusual display, he tried a few buttons before figuring out what he needed, then quickly put the net down.

Bolt pointed his wand under his cart. "*Laaloopikaatilo!*[6]" he yelled. Noctus relaxed and stopped fighting. Bolt rolled him off the cage and to the ground below. He flew his cart beside Noctus and rolled him into the net.

Bolt stick-hopped to Subter. He was moaning and beginning to move. "*Laaloopikaatilo!*" he repeated. Subter stopped moving. Bolt and Bug rolled him into the net beside Noctus.

"Where did you learn those spells?" asked Rey.

"You saw me in the library," answered Bolt. "Now see if you can wrap your defense nets around those two."

"Who put you in charge?" said Rey. But she reached for her s'more pouch. "I can't get my pouch opened."

Bolt tried his pouch. It wouldn't open either. "Anybody able to get their pouch open?"

"No," answered Bug, Lil, and Scout in unison.

Rey shook her head, seemingly frustrated that Bolt was calling the shots. "Watch this," she said. She produced her wand and pointed it at the net. "*Kchiptilo!*[7]" she

---

[6] Paralyze! - swinging legs (laah-loo-pee-kaah-tee-lo)

[7] Tie up! (kcheep-tee-lo)

pronounced. The net coiled into loops and tightened around the two stratoids like a boa constrictor.

"Impressive," said Bolt.

"Thank you," said Rey, looking surprised that Bolt had paid her a compliment.

"Okay, Scout," said Bolt, "raise that net as high as the boom will take it."

Scout put the boom into full extension, holding the net against a thirty-foot ceiling. "That's as high as she'll go."

"Okay," said Bolt, "let's get out of here."

The Mad River Magic gang hopped into their carts and set off, away from the truck. Bolt had no idea where they were going. He looked back at the two stratoids, dangling in the tight net like a spider's web. Somehow he knew they would be freed soon. The gang had better hurry.

Initially the gang flew in two clusters, Bolt and Scout on one side, Rey and the girls on the other. The two groups quickly merged. Bolt glanced at Rey, who flew beside him. Could they cooperate to succeed in getting out of here?

One hundred yards away from the truck, he noticed faint lines of light under the dust on the floor. He set down his cart. When he rubbed away the dust, road lines appeared. Below the road lines, the floor felt and looked like acrylic glass, smooth and flexible, yeah, like the Plexiglas backboards on the basketball courts back home. And this stuff was apparently transmitting the gray light that surrounded them. Was that another space below the road? Strange. Well, this road had to lead somewhere.

They set off again, following the road lines that led into the gray haze. As they traveled, a brighter light began to appear in the distance. It, too, was gray, but shining. Something lay ahead. Bolt swallowed hard and led the way.

As the five flying carts zipped along just below the ceiling, the gang surveyed their new surroundings. Scout looked around, eyes wide open in amazement. Rey held her wand at ready, prepared for whatever monster might materialize. Lil tearfully stayed close to Rey, repeating, "When are we going home?" And Bug swooped and dived, delighting in her new environment to do aerial acrobatics.

The weight of responsibility was beginning to settle on Bolt. Looking around at the gang, it was obvious. They would look to him for leadership. He was the oldest. Rey led the girls, and she often clashed with him. But they would need to work together if they were to ever escape this nightmare.

Bolt turned his cart and led the way toward the gray light.

As they approached the distant target, unusual objects began to appear out of the fog. A large transparent horizontal tube suddenly appeared on the floor to the right of the road lights and parallel to the road. Dark gray objects, moving so fast he couldn't make them out, whizzed past inside the tube. Within minutes they reached similar tubes criss-crossing the floor below them. Then vertical hollow columns sprouted, like pillars supporting the ceiling. But as Bolt watched the flying objects inside the vertical columns, he noticed that they pierced the floor and the ceiling, and the columns extended into layers above and below them. What was this strange place?

The eerie gray light ahead became brighter and seemed to be much closer now. Looking down, Bolt noticed activity. At first it looked like baseball diamonds dotting the floor below. But as he skirted one area to remain unnoticed, he observed that what he thought was an infield was actually an empty stage. The movement coming from people, probably stratoids, was not lining the first base and third base lines, but was actually coming from the edges of that stage. The line of stratoids on one side was light gray. Dark gray stratoids lined the other side. Both groups seemed to be waving their arms and yelling to invisible actors on the empty stage.

Bolt rubbed his eyes. Yeah, he was awake. Wow, this was weird.

Next, box-like buildings sprouted up below them. They must be approaching a city. The light was brighter and less gray, but Bolt still couldn't see the source.

Before he realized what he had done, he found himself and the gang directly over an empty stage. Blast. The directors on the light line waved. Those on the dark line pointed and yelled. He didn't know what they were yelling, but he knew it wasn't good. They'd better find a place to hide.

An intersecting road presented itself below them. Bolt turned and followed the side road, inspecting the warehouse-like boxes on either side, looking for a hiding place.

He maneuvered his cart beside Rey. "I think we need to find a place to hide," said Bolt. "That group back there noticed us, and someone is likely to report us."

Rey nodded in agreement and pointed to a building. The parking lot was empty. A fence surrounded the lot, and the gate was chained and locked. The windows were dark.

"Let's do it," said Bolt. And he led the group over the fence.

They set down their carts in front of a large industrial door. A big dusty padlock hung from the door.

"Can you open that?" asked Bolt.

Rey pulled out her wand. Before she said anything, a screeching whistle filled the air.

"Siren," said Bolt. "Quick, open the door."

Rey pointed her wand at the padlock. "*Tawenehilo!*[8]" yelled Rey.

The padlock snapped open.

But before the gang could open the door, a huge cage truck hovered over them and a beam of darkness enveloped them so that they couldn't see.

"Don't move!" boomed a large voice from above.

---

[8] Unlock! (tah-way-nay-hee-lo)

"Let's get out of here," yelled Bolt. He couldn't see, but he flew his cart away from the building and was immediately out of the darkness. Looking back over his shoulder, he saw the gang following him. And behind them the cage truck was giving chase.

Bolt pushed his turbos to full throttle. The buildings below began to flash past more quickly. He thought the rest of the gang was keeping up. But when he glanced back, Rey and Lil were lagging, and the cage truck was right on their tail. Oh, blast. What now?

He heard the girls screaming. As he turned to aim his wand at the truck, he heard shouts from below. Looking down, he found himself over another empty stage, light stratoids again on one side, dark ones on the other side. The light stratoids were pointing up, at something ahead of him. The dark startoids were laughing and waving him on.

Bolt turned back to see what the light stratoids were pointing at, just in time to slam into a clear plastic wall. He managed to stay in his cart as it slid down the partition that reached from floor to ceiling. The rest of the gang skidded to a stop and avoided injury, setting their carts down beside Bolt.

The truck was closing in fast. What now?

"Hey," said Scout, pointing to their right, "there's an alley over there"

The gang zoomed into the passageway. Something didn't feel right. The truck followed. And sure enough, a hundred yards in they hit a dead end. Bolt looked up, expecting the truck to hit them with a black beam. Nothing.

Bolt was rubbing his head, contemplating their next move, when a door opened.

Snap. Bang. There was no time to react. The gang was sucked into a large horizontal tube, like the ones they had seen crisscrossing the Strata along the road. The door snapped shut, and they were accelerated into blurring speed, all in the time it took Bolt to blink.

He checked to make sure the gang was together. Lil was crying again. Scout's eyes were bigger than ever. Bug looked around to see what was coming next. And Rey held her wand out, yelling, "*Teki!*[9]" But nothing stopped, and they were sucked away at gut-wrenching speed.

Bolt yelled to the group, "Stay in your carts," and then realized that he didn't need to yell. Their speedy travel was silent. Looking out through the transparent tube, he saw gray blurs whiz by, but couldn't tell what he was seeing.

Where were they going? He felt so helpless.

Five minutes into their travel, the gang came to a sudden stop. A click beside them accompanied a large door popping open. And in another blink of an eye they

---

[9] Stop! (tay'kee)

were sitting outside the horizontal tube. The door closed as soon as it opened. They rubbed their eyes, getting their bearings.

"Let's get out—" Bolt started to say, when a click above them made them look up. But by the time they looked, they were already inside a vertical column, the door had closed behind them, and they were hurtled straight up. Bolt wanted to vomit, but his stomach was empty.

Once again, the group was together. Bug was the only one who seemed to be enjoying this terror ride. Bolt now realized that someone was controlling this sinister game of tubes and columns. And he was pretty certain that it was one of the dark guys.

His heart was racing. Sweat covered his forehead. What did this evil one have planned for them?

Chapter Ten

Extor's Palace of Night

*B*olt looked up as the gang rose vertically at break-neck speed. The column above them was closed. Bolt braced for the crash. But the top silently opened, and the gang found themselves in a large room. Surrounding the gang stood a ring of silent dark-gray stratoid guards with folded arms and big frowns on their hazy translucent faces.

Bolt surveyed the room. On one side sat a large desk below a sign that read, "Visitor Reception Center." The ceiling was a translucent shiny gray, revealing blurry figures walking around above them. The floor was similar to the road they had first encountered when they entered the Strata. The walls appeared to be the source of a bright gray light that radiated from them, and everything was covered in shades of gray. How depressing.

A door opened in one wall, ushering in the largest, darkest, ugliest, creature of the night that Bolt had ever seen. Peals of thunder and flashes of gray light announced his entrance. Bolt shuddered. The gang huddled together. This stratoid was shaped like the others, but larger, and he had sharp jagged, almost furry, features that reminded Bolt of a coyote and a badger blended into a single mass of evil. His eyes shone like coals with flickers of gray flashing fire .

Unlike the uniform the other stratoids wore, this apparent leader was wrapped in a continuous swath of black cloth, like a toga ending in a hood that covered his hair. Only his face pierced the gray light. His hands projected out from the dark cloth, long and thin, with dirty black fingernails. And on his forehead, branded in black, was an apple. An aura of darkness that inhibited light penetration surrounded him.

The ring of guards bowed and floated back, allowing this creature of the night to step into the center and in front of the gang. They cowered toward the other side of the ring.

"Welcome to the Visitor Reception Center," boomed a resonant bass voice. "I am Extor, Prince of Night, your host for your stay here in the Strata. You will refer to me as The Prince."

Bolt looked at the others. Scout was pressed up against him. The girls were huddled around Rey. He swallowed hard and looked back at Extor, but couldn't meet his eyes.

"I hope your stay with us will be pleasant," continued Extor. "And I trust there will be no further attempt at escape." He stopped to laugh so loudly the room seemed to reverberate with a blast of thunder. "I do want to thank you for giving my men some practice in retrieval and containment. They were due for a search and rescue drill. And poor Subter and Noctus, after they've hung from their cocoon for a few days, I don't think they will ever be so careless again."

The ring of guards chuckled. Extor's glare stopped them instantly.

"I know who you are," said Extor. "I've been seeking subjects from your neck of the woods, as you call it, for a long time. You see, your grandfather, or at least his predecessor, and I have some history between us. But enough of that. You will be very important ambassadors to your home and your grandfather after you have finished your training here. I hope, at that point, you will finally see the night. I have tried to work with one of your neighbors, but that individual has been uncooperative."

Extor rubbed his translucent chin with his scrawny fingers, contemplating silently for a second. "But your cap...arrival will change everything. I believe there will be reason for us to negotiate."

"So now," boomed Extor, as he clapped his hands twice and his guards came to attention, "it is time for your tour, and then you will be shown to your quarters. I think you will find that everything here is most luxurious, and you will want for nothing. Your carts will be secured in our containment center, so there will be no temptation to leave us. And I suggest that you begin sleeping during the light hours. Your lessons and meals will be during the time of darkness, the hours of greatest potential."

Extor spun and departed the room as quickly as he had entered, by simply fading and disappearing. All but four of the guards followed him.

The leader of the four remaining stratoids turned to the gang. "Follow me," he said in a raspy voice. "And don't try anything stupid, or you will pay dearly." A sinister grin appeared on his face.

He moved toward a double door that led into a hallway. The three remaining guards flanked and followed the gang. Mad River Magic huddled close together.

Bolt moved to the front of the gang so that he could see in both directions. The wide hallway was lined with doors on both sides. As they walked quickly, the leading guard encouraged them to look through the windows into the rooms and notice the luxurious furnishings. Indeed, the rooms had large beds, beautiful pictures on the walls, a comfortable sitting area with a big table, and a wide screen TV. But everything was gray. And Bolt noticed that all doors were closed and locked with a sliding bolt mounted on the hallway side. Beside each door, a small sign stated a language, from English to multiple unrecognizable languages.

The people in the rooms were doing enjoyable things, stretched out on the bed watching TV, eating a large meal at the table, reading, even snoozing. Yet all the prisoners looked worried and unhappy. He didn't see a single smile. And no one seemed to be enjoying any of the supposedly enjoyable things they were doing.

Walking past one room, he got just a glance of a single male prisoner. Mr. Finkelstein. No, it couldn't be. He looked back, but it was too late. Glancing at the rest of the gang, it didn't appear that anyone else had noticed. He looked back one more time. Room 262.

The guard stopped at a laundry area and handed each member of the gang a folded uniform. One by one they were sent into the room to change. Their regular clothes and their s'more packs were confiscated, and the gang was told that the clothing would be returned when they had successfully completed their indoctrination. While Bolt was changing, he noticed a single small window, high on the back wall. An opaque service door on the same wall was closed and secured with three heavy locks.

As each member of the gang took their turn at changing, Bolt silently mouthed "wand," reminding them to keep and hide their only weapon.

Mad River Magic now wore their first uniforms, prison garb or scrub suits, depending on one's outlook. The pants were held with a drawstring and had one pocket in the back. The tops had a V-neck, and a single pocket that was too small for their wands. Bolt had tied his inside his drawstring and covered it with the front of his top. A variegated design covered the uniforms, apples in all shades of gray.

Looking around at the rest of the gang, Bolt sensed the humiliation and fear. Those emotions sat heavy on his heart, as well, but something had to be done to protect his friends' spirit. He and Rey would need to work together. Bitten lower lips and near-tears were not going to get them out of here.

"Cool outfit, Rey," said Bolt with a tight grin and a nod.

She started to say something, then nodded with a glance, agreeing to a truce. "Why, thank you," said Rey, as she curtsied.

Bug and Lil turned pirouettes, and Scout's wide eyes decreased by one size as he began exploring his surroundings. With a faint tight smile, Bolt gave Rey a single quick nod. They could do this.

"Enough of this stupid play!" barked the raspy-voiced guard. And he was on his way down the long hallway again. The three other guards pushed the gang to keep up.

Bolt studied the solid bar of gray light on the ceiling. He could imagine Scout dissecting it, exploring the source of energy. Bolt studied the hallway in more detail, shiny, opaque gray curved at the bottom to blend with the floor. It reminded him of his first steps in the bowl trap.

Halfway down the hall, a flight of steps went up and down. Beside the steps stood a doorway to a vertical tube. Bolt wanted to check the controls for the number of floors in the building, but a guard remained between him and the wall.

At the far end of the hall two large doors opened into what appeared to be a huge classroom. Row after row of desks and chairs were arranged in a multi-layered amphitheater-type setting. Wow, this place could hold over a thousand people. Bolt noticed a switch on the desk where each occupant could select their language. The guard proudly led them down the steps to the front stage, rattling off all the state-of-the-art audiovisuals this auditorium contained, but Bolt's attention was drawn to a large map on the wall at the back of the stage.

"The Strata" was printed at the top of the map. On stage, Bolt inched closer and tried to take in every detail. He was prevented from approaching the map by the guards, but he did see that the map shaded from dark to light. In the middle of the top was a large circle that stated simply "Omni." On the light side was an apparent small town that said "Palace of Light." And on the dark side was a huge area, and apparent city, that was labeled in large proud letters, "Extor's Palace of Night." In the triangular area in the middle, there appeared to be symbols for trees. Hmm. That was the first sign he'd seen of plant life.

"Young man," said the raspy guard, "pay attention." He glanced at the map Bolt had been studying. "That's simply a map of the fantasy history of this area." He flipped a switch, and the map disappeared.

"This auditorium," continued the guard, "is where your education will take place. Classes begin promptly at midnight, daily. You will receive a wake-up call at 10 p.m. Your first meal of the day will be served at 11 p.m. And your doors will be opened at 11:45 p.m. so that you can be in your seats and ready for your lessons by midnight. You will discover that being on time is highly advisable. We start promptly at midnight, and we take tardiness very seriously. After missing meals for a day, I don't think you will be late again." He smiled as he looked at each member of the gang.

"When you find a seat," said the guard, "move this switch until it displays 'English.' "He pointed at the small screen built into each desk.

Bolt watched the guard, but his mind was contemplating how he could make a copy of the map at the back of the stage. He was beginning to formulate a plan. Yeah, he really needed to study that map.

"One final thought before I take you to your room," said the guard. "I will give you a warning. You won't hear this again, or from anyone else." He rubbed his hands together and smiled gleefully. "You would do well to take your lessons seriously and make a true change of heart. We will know if you don't. And those who don't, well, let me just say that those failures are taken to a secret location where the essence of free will is removed from their mind and heart, and they are returned to their *real world*, as you call it, as an unexplained death." He squinted fiercely at the gang. "Don't let that be you."

Chapter Eleven

Prisoners in Dark Paradise

Ten minutes later the gang was shut into their room on the third floor. The guard had left, sliding the lock on the outside of the door firmly into place.

As they had walked from the auditorium to their room, Bolt had studied the security carefully. Hopping up the steps, he had noticed that the third floor was the top floor, at least as far as the staircase went. A laundry room similar to the one on the second floor appeared to sit directly above the one on the second floor. And he had been totally amazed when they were ushered into Room 362, apparently directly over Room 262. Was this a trap?

The gang explored their prison room carefully. Actually their "suite" included a common room, two bedrooms, and a shared bathroom. Bolt looked around the ceilings and didn't see any surveillance cameras, but whispered to each gang member to keep their wands hidden. He and Rey then used their covered wands to search for bugs. Once located, they set up wands to emit interfering white noise.

Now they could talk and plan. They huddled in a corner farthest from the bugs.

"Okay," said Bolt. "What do you think?"

"I say we bust out of here as soon as possible," said Rey. "I think we can open the lock on the outside of our room. You saw the locks on the door in the laundry room. We can open those as well."

"Then what?" asked Bolt.

"Then we find the containment center," said Bug, "take our carts, and get out of here."

"And where do we go?" asked Bolt.

"I want to go home," said Lil. "Let's go back to Gram and Gramps and Mom and Dad." Rey put her arm around Lil's shoulders.

"What do you think, Scout?" asked Bolt.

Scout looked around at the strange surroundings. "I would like to explore how these lights work, what their source of energy is," he said. "If there is any way we can tap into that, it could be very useful for our escape."

"So you're in favor of sticking around and learning more about this place?" asked Bolt.

"Yeah, I guess," said Scout.

The girls didn't look too happy with the direction the plan was going.

"Does anyone have any ideas for where we would go after we escape?" asked Bolt.

Everyone shook their heads.

"I don't know either," said Bolt, "but that map at the back of the auditorium stage may be our best clue. Did you see the small town on the light side of the map, Palace of Light? If it's the opposite of this place, it would be a good place to start."

"But how do we get there?" asked Rey.

"I don't know yet," answered Bolt, "but I would like to figure out how to make a copy of that map so we can study it."

"I still say we get out of here now," said Bug. "I can't stand this place."

"One more thing," said Bolt. "Did anyone notice the prisoner in Room 262?"

Apparently no one had, based on their confused looks.

"Mr. Finkelstein," said Bolt. "He's in the room right below this one."

"But how—" began Rey.

"I don't know," said Bolt, "but maybe we can get some information from him. Maybe he can help us, or maybe..." He paused. "Maybe we should help him escape."

"No!" answered the gang in unison.

Bolt shrugged his shoulders. "Well, let's at least hang around for another day or two to learn how this place operates and to plan our escape."

The girls grumbled. Scout began looking at the light fixtures.

Bolt sat at the table, thinking how he could make a copy of the map. And was there a way to communicate with Finkelstein? Or would Finkelstein blow their cover? Could he be a plant? He moved to the big screen TV and explored the back.

"Now what?" asked Rey. "What will Extor demand of us?"

Bolt rubbed the white hair that refused to stay combed. Yeah, what now? Why did this have to be so complicated? "I have no idea. But I don't think we'll want to do it." He turned back to the TV.

"Hey, Bolt," called Scout. "Look at this."

Scout was in the bathroom with the dismantled light bar spread out on the counter in front of him. Wires and screws were everywhere. Bolt shook his head, grinning. Leave it to Scout.

"Look," said Scout. The excitement in his voice betrayed his pride as he held up a cube and a glowing gray wire. "This diode is powered by this cube. And the cube is not connected to any energy source. It's portable."

"That's great," said Bolt. "We'll take that with us when we escape. Now let's all get some sleep so we're ready for tomorrow. Midnight will come too soon."

With all the excitement, he doubted that any of them could sleep, but they turned off the lights. His mind continued to work on a way to copy that map.

Chapter Twelve

Lessons in Evil

The box on the desk began ringing at 10:00 p.m., the ringing quickly turned into music, and then the voice started.

Bug threw her pillow at the wake-up call and rolled over in bed. Rey was already up and getting dressed. Lil clung to Rey. And Scout was studying the box. Bolt walked out to the common area and listened.

A syrupy-sweet female voice began. "Good evening, visitors. It is time to rise and begin the most influential part of the night. Please clean up quickly. Breakfast will be served in one hour. Your room will be opened at 11:45 p.m., when you will proceed to the auditorium where your instruction will begin. If this is your first night here at our reception center, you will find your books and study supplies stacked on your desk. Please bring them with you to the lectures. You would be wise to protect your materials from injury, because obvious abuse of your materials will result in being collared and spending an appropriate period of time in the containment center. And, I would add, failure to arrive at the lecture sessions in a timely manner will also result in similar corrective action.

"So, dear guests, prepare to learn. Let's fight the light. Let's see the night."

"What was that?" said Bug.

Bolt quickly silenced her with a hand over her mouth, pointing at the hidden microphones. Rey and Bolt reset the white noise, and the group huddled again in the far corner.

"Okay, gang," said Bolt. "Let's get ready. Don't believe anything you hear today, but learn what you can. Be alert for information that will be helpful in our escape. Stay together and put on your happy faces." He lifted the corners of Lil's mouth into a smile.

She slapped away his hand, but there was a grin behind that frown. If they could just keep their spirits up, they might have a chance.

Bolt and Scout checked the stacks of books. They sat neatly on the desk. Someone had entered their room last night. What else had they done or observed? Each stack included a pouch with a set of headphones and a separate device that looked like ear muffs. Scout already had the headphones plugged into the jack on the TV and was listening.

"Anything?" asked Bolt.

"No," answered Scout. "It sounds like someone's setting up the stage."

Bolt walked to the window and peered outside. The same dim gray light permeated everything. Oh, it was so depressing. Back home, this dreary weather would look like rain was on the way. If he made it back, he would never complain about rain again.

The gang hustled to get cleaned up. At precisely 11:00 p.m. the lock clicked, the door opened, and a cart with five trays was pushed to their table by a small light-gray stratoid. Bolt hadn't seen this size of stratoid before. He, she? He couldn't tell. It wore the same uniform as the guards, but lighter. Dark piercing eyes shone out from fuzzy translucent facial features. Bolt watched for any emotion, but saw none. The stratoid said nothing and made no eye contact. It quickly set each tray on the table and turned to leave.

"Thanks," said Bolt.

The stratoid turned to Bolt, eyes cast down, and in a hushed child-like voice said, "You are welcome." Then it turned to leave.

Bolt still wasn't sure whether this was life or machine. "Will, you be back tomorrow?" he asked.

And without stopping or turning, the stratoid responded, "Yes, I will return."

The door closed. The lock clicked. Bolt observed that the door had been open, unguarded, for about two minutes.

The gang sat down to eat. Bolt wasn't about to pretend to be religious, but silently breathed a prayer. Back at Cedar Heights, at the kitchen table, he had heard Gram and Gramps ask for strength. He and the gang sure could use some of that right now.

As the gang began eating, Bolt realized that this meal was the first thing in the Strata that he had seen that wasn't gray. The orange juice was orange. The eggs were yellow. The sausage was brown. The grape jelly was purple. Wow! He sniffed. The meal even had smell. Yum, he was hungry.

After breakfast, Bolt and Rey gave final instructions to the gang, then collected the wands. Each member secured their wand beneath their clothing. They were ready, he hoped.

At 11:45 p.m. the doors popped open, and the gang joined the river of prisoners—visitors, Bolt reminded himself—flowing down the wide hallway toward the auditorium. The uniforms, with their hemlock apples, and the gray light bar overhead created a smothering weight that pressed on Bolt's chest. It reminded him of the compression he felt when the gang first entered the Strata.

The redheads, blonds, and brunettes provided the only color to the dirty gray stream. As he looked closer, he noticed that a majority of the females wore dark gray make-up, had dyed their hair black, and sported shiny black fingernails. He glanced at Rey. She had seen it, too. He rubbed his white bolt of hair, trying to make it lie down. It wouldn't, and suddenly he felt like a lightning rod drawing attention. He needed some red hair dye. There was no way he would ever dye his hair black. He tried to keep his crutches from getting tangled in the mass around him.

Going past the laundry room, he noticed that some of the prisoners were dropping off large bags stuffed with dirty uniforms. Behind the half door, a dark stratoid was stacking the bags along a wall. No one else was in that room, but the back door stood open.

As they hit the bottom of the staircase and merged with the...visitors...from the second floor, the hallway became tighter and the flow slowed. Bolt looked around for Mr. Finkelstein. He didn't see old Fink, but he saw his first collared prisoner. Choke-collar-type chain around her neck, head down in embarrassment, and hands cuffed behind her, the fiery redhead shuffled forward through the throng, pushed forward by the large dark-gray stratoid behind her. Everyone in the hallway moved out of the way as she was forced toward the stairway. Bolt's stomach tightened. They were parading her down the hall as a warning to everyone else. They could have moved her at a different time. He felt his blood pressure rise.

Behind the lead collared prisoner followed a string of about ten other examples. Bolt clenched his fist. He felt Rey's hand on his shoulder. Man, these creatures were going to pay for this.

And then emotion punched him in the gut twice as hard. The last prisoner, old and frail, hair gray and uncombed, passed immediately beside Bolt. Pushed by his guard until he would stumble, the collared prisoner was then jerked back up. The prisoner stumbled again. Bolt reached out reflexly to catch him.

"Don't touch him!" commanded the guard.

The prisoner's eyes met Bolt's. Mr. Finkelstein! Bolt's mouth went dry, and he couldn't say anything.

Mr. Finkelstein's eyes shone with tears. He shook his head almost imperceptibly. And he silently mouthed, "No."

Bolt looked away.

The parade passed as the collared prisoners turned and went down the stairway. The river of visitors merged and flowed again toward the auditorium. Bolt couldn't get his mind off Mr. Finkelstein. Why was he here in the first place? And what had he done that caused him to be collared?

When the gang passed through the auditorium doors, the other prisoners—he just couldn't bring himself to call them visitors—made a bee line for specific seats. Bolt shook his head. This wasn't like going to the movies. A back row seat would be just fine.

The gang looked around for five seats together and warily took their places. After turning the language switch to English, they put on their headphones. The auditorium filled quickly. Apparently no one wanted to sport a collar tomorrow.

Then the headphones filled with music. It was instantly hypnotic. Bolt shook his head to stay focused. The instructor walked onto the stage, and his voice took the lead while the hypnotherapy filled the background. Bolt glanced at the rest of the gang to make sure no one's eyes were glazing over. This place was really something.

"Welcome, visitors," said the large stratoid at the podium. His features were fuzzy like the others, but he looked closer to human form than any other stratoid Bolt had seen thus far. A dark gray uniform covered him like a tailor-made suit, and his voice resonated with the authority of a politician.

"Tonight we are going to review several lessons before we move on to new material," said the professor. "First we will look again at the benefits of Night Life. Then I'll give you an overview of the training you will receive here at the Visitors' Center. And finally we will focus on your mission, once you reenter the surface world."

Bolt looked around at the rest of the auditorium. Yep, the women were leaning forward in their seats, taking in every word, especially those with black makeup.

"Now, who can list for me the top five benefits of a life lived at night, avoiding the danger of light?" asked the professor.

Hands shot up around the auditorium, waving, begging for attention. The middle-aged lady who was called on swayed as she answered the question. "Number one, enjoy all earthly pleasures. No need for sacrifice or delayed gratification.

"Number two, make your own rules. Do what *you* want. Put yourself first. Take what you want. Number three, hide what you want to hide. No punishment. Number four, ignore what you don't want to see. No need for guilt or responsibility.

"And number five, discover how easy it is to influence others to follow you. Get what you want from them." She heaved a sigh, smiled, and sat down.

"Very good, Mrs. Sponge," said the professor. "Word for word from the textbook. Let's all give her a round of applause."

"Next," continued the professor, "who can explain to any new members, the goal of our training here and the purpose of our return to the surface world?"

Again, hands shot up throughout the auditorium. The young lady who was chosen wore an unsmiling face and spoke in monotone.

"Our goal here," she answered, "is to learn how we can be the strongest force for darkness, as an extension of Extor's coaches. Our purpose, when we return to the surface world, is to help people there tune into that inner voice that is one of Extor's coaches."

"Very good," said the professor.

Bolt took a deep breath. How was he going to make it through a whole night of this? He glanced at Lil. Was she tough enough? She grinned back at him. He winked. They could do this.

He felt in his back pocket to make certain the chip was still there. Now just stay awake until the lunch break.

The professor droned on in his honey-sweet voice. The background music rose and fell as if a conductor watched from the orchestra pit. Bolt reviewed his plan over and over to keep himself awake.

When the lunch break finally arrived, the ladies in black swarmed the podium.

"Come on, Scout," said Bolt. "We're on."

They fought their way through the throng. At the podium, Bolt handed off the chip and covered while Scout ducked below to the computer. When he popped back up, they moved toward the professor, where the women were asking questions.

"Sir," asked Bolt, "could you give us a little history of the beautiful map that sometimes adorns the back of the stage."

At first the professor looked surprised that someone other than a woman in black was asking a question, but then he caught himself. "Certainly, young man," answered the professor. He glanced at the back wall and moved to the podium to turn on the map.

"This map is a rendition of the Strata, outside of The Palace of Night..." he hesitated. "Er, the fantasy history of this world. The village named Palace of Light and the circle marked Omni don't actually exist. Legend has it that when The Prince of Night, Extor, came to the Strata, he had to do battle with the ruler, Omni, and his daughter, the Princess of Light. Once they were vanquished, the Strata was ruled by The Prince of Night." The professor glanced nervously at the guards standing by the doors at the back of the auditorium as he turned away from Bolt.

But Bolt continued. "Do those villages still exist today?"

Barely turning toward Bolt, the professor turned off the map and answered, "No, they were completely destroyed. Now, any other questions?"

Hmm, Bolt thought for a second, they didn't actually exist, but they were completely destroyed. He turned to find Scout, who had just popped up from the podium computer.

"Got it," said Scout, tapping his pants pocket. "Now let's get out of here."

They followed the other visitors to their seats, where lunch trays had already been placed. Bolt wasn't really hungry, but the color in the food was a welcome change from everything else gray. Where was the Strata growing or getting this food? It just wasn't natural to get hungry in the middle of the night.

He kept thinking about the map, eager to get back to their room and explore it. Was it possible that there really were other areas of the Strata that were controlled by beings other than Extor? And what would they be like? Anything would be better than this. Did they have enough information to break out and try to find their way to the Palace of Light?

Throughout the afternoon lectures the questions kept rolling over and over in his mind. He checked every thirty minutes or so to make sure no one in the gang was being hypnotized, then returned to his rumination. What would they do about Finkelstein? They couldn't leave him here to be tortured by Extor. Bolt never thought he would have any sympathy for Mr. Fink. If they could just communicate with him...

At the end of the afternoon all the prisoners were instructed to place the other device, the ear muffs, over their temples, to "reinforce" what they had learned today. Bolt looked around at the rest of the auditorium. Everyone else was complying. He nodded to the gang, and they all placed on their reinforcers. He didn't like this. What was really being done? He wanted to get back to the room and study the map.

After ten minutes of this worthless exercise, they were allowed to remove the pads and the earphones and return to their room. No parade of collared prisoners appeared during the gang's return trip. What were the guards doing to the prisoners in the containment center? And where exactly was the containment center?

When the gang reached Room 362, the door, unlike those to the other rooms, stood open.

Chapter Thirteen

Into the Depths of Darkness

Mad River Magic entered cautiously. In front of the wide screen TV stood two dark gray stratoids. And they weren't smiling.

"Line up!" commanded one of the guards.

Something told Bolt to stand next to Scout.

"As our guests, we have provided you with every possible amenity to make your stay more enjoyable," said one of the stratoids. "But you have betrayed us." He paused and searched each of their faces. "Do you know what I am talking about?"

The gang looked at each other in confusion. Bolt moved closer to Scout and put his hands behind his back.

"We know that you have taken the memory chip from the wide screen," continued the stratoid. "Will one of you confess to the theft, or would all of you like to spend tonight in collars?"

Scouts eyes widened. He slipped the chip from his pants pocket and held his hands behind his back.

The stratoid looked at him.

Bolt grabbed the chip from Scout's hands and swung forward. "I have it." He held it out to the stratoid.

The stratoid glared at Scout, then took the chip from Bolt.

"Your punishment for the theft," said the stratoid, addressing Bolt, "will be to spend this coming night collared and with nothing to eat or drink. And as an extra measure, to make an impression on your young friend," he glared at Scout, "you will also spend today in cuffs." He glanced at Bolt's crutches. "Turn around."

Bolt turned, and the stratoid placed the cuffs on Bolt's ankles.

"I don't know why we're giving you a pass," said the stratoid. "I would have put these on your wrists, but I'm not in charge around here." He frowned and shook his head.

After the stratoids strode out of the room and the door slammed, Lil broke into tears. The gang circled Bolt.

"I'm sorry," said Rey.

Scout's head hung down, his lips quivered.

"Hey, it was my idea," said Bolt. "It's okay,"

Bolt motioned to Rey to check for any new bugs and set up white noise, while he stick-hopped around the room looking for any cameras. The group then huddled for their strategy session.

"Look," said Rey, "we can get these cuffs off and unlock the door. We don't have the map, but we got a look at it today. I studied it while the professor had it on. I say we break out, find the containment center, get our carts, and head for the Palace of Light."

"Yeah, let's go for it," said Bug.

Lil clung to Rey, not saying anything.

"What do you think?" asked Scout, looking at Bolt.

"I'm as eager to get out of here as the rest of you," said Bolt. "But we have the opportunity to learn exactly where the containment center is, and hopefully, to locate our carts. And I want to talk to Mr. Finkelstein, if he's in the containment center tonight, to help us decide what we do with him."

"What?" said Rey. "I thought you couldn't stand the guy."

"Things are different now," answered Bolt. "We have a responsibility to help him. And he might have some information that would help all of us."

"I don't like the idea," said Rey.

"We're in agreement that we need to make it to the Palace of Light," said Bolt. "Even if Finkelstein doesn't go with us, he might be able to help us."

"I agree with Bolt," said Scout.

"Okay," said Rey, with disappointment. "The rest of us will gather as much information as possible. I have an idea."

"What?" asked Bug.

"I need to think about it today," she answered. "I'll tell you when we get up."

"Oh, one more thing," said Bolt. "Those reinforcer pads we put on at the end of the lecture. They may have been collecting data, our thoughts, not reinforcing data. Tonight, at the end of the session, everyone get out one of the books and read continuously until the pads come off. Don't think for even one second about our plans. Keep your thoughts on the book. Got it?"

The gang all nodded in agreement.

Bolt sat on the edge of his bed. At least they had a plan now. Do or die, they had no choice. They had to get out of here. They had to make it to The Palace of Light. That was their only hope. And Finkelstein, well, he could decide whether or not he wanted to come with them. Bolt breathed another prayer, "Help us make the right decisions."

That night, Bolt woke up with a sore back from being unable to move his legs. When he hopped out to the common space to check on the rest of the gang, his books had been replaced by a choke collar. He sat and inspected its construction.

The 10 p.m. wake-up call brought the room to life. As the rest of the gang groaned and crawled out of bed, Bolt moved to the window to see if anything had changed. It hadn't. The same dark gray light greeted him and added to his sadness. Looking at the ground below the window, he saw no activity.

When he turned back to the room, he almost choked. Rey stood outside the bathroom waiting for his attention. Her hair was black. Dark gray make-up smeared her face, running down in tears below her eyes, and shiny black paint glistened on her nails. She held her hands above her head and spun for his inspection.

Bolt opened his mouth to demand an explanation, but Rey quickly held a finger to her closed lips. After looking around to be certain that the wands were in place, Bolt hopped past Rey, jerking his head for her to follow him to their conference area. He wanted to grab her by the shoulder and drag her. What was she doing!

"Before you get angry," began Rey, "hear me out."

Bolt sat back with a grimace and squint. This better be good.

"While you're doing your research today," said Rey, "I'm going to see what I can dig up."

"So why the black and gray makeup?" asked Bolt.

"You saw the swooners last night," said Rey. "They're obviously not scrutinized as carefully as the rest of us."

"So what are you trying to find?" asked Bolt.

"Let me surprise you." She grinned.

"Swooners don't smile or grin," said Bolt. "Don't blow your cover today." He turned to walk back to the common room, then stopped. "Oh, you better hide in the bathroom while they bring in our breakfast. We'll confuse the server with a groupie and a rebel both in the same group. It was friendly last night. We don't want to blow any chance of assistance."

At 10:55 p.m. Rey disappeared into the bathroom, and the rest of the gang assembled at the breakfast table. At precisely 11:00 p.m. the lock clicked, the door opened, and the same small stratoid pushed a cart containing four breakfast trays.

Knowing that he would get no food, Bolt pushed his chair back from the table. The server placed the four trays on the table. It was a she. Long hair poked out from under her cap.

She turned to Bolt, a tear in her eye. "I am not permitted to give you any food. I am sorry." Stepping closer, she placed a card in his hand, then quickly left the room.

Bolt held the card under the table and read quickly. "Benecia, assistant to Solia, Princess of Light," then an address. He slipped the card into his pocket. Where could he hide this?

Although not really hungry at 11:00 p.m., Bolt moved away from the table. He didn't want to be tempted.

Scout offered him a fork full of pancakes.

"Thanks," said Bolt, shaking his head, then whispered to Scout, "Somehow, I think they would know." He moved from the table and sat at the desk.

Rey emerged from the bathroom and sat at the table to eat her breakfast. The rest of the gang ignored her, except Lil, who kept looking at her in disbelief.

At 11:45 p.m. the lock clicked and the door popped open. But this time a dark stratoid entered.

"Wise decision," said the stratoid, addressing Bolt. "If you would have eaten, your time of collaring would have been doubled." And looking at Scout, "If there is one more episode of attempted disobedience, you will be punished as well. You will find that Extor demands perfect allegiance. Those who transgress repeatedly are...let's just say that their free will plasma is removed and their empty body is returned to the surface world as a..."

He turned again to Bolt. "You will learn all those details tonight."

The gang hung their heads and glanced at Bolt. He held his head up and put his shoulders back, staring at each gang member until they held up their head and smiled.

"Don't get any ideas, boys and girls," said the stratoid. Then, admiring Rey's make-up, he added, "I see at least one of you is beginning to see the night. Wise choice, young lady."

The stratoid fastened the choke collar and pushed Bolt out the door. Bolt fell into the chain gang line right behind Mr. Finkelstein. Good, he would find a way to communicate with him tonight.

The collared prisoners marched down the hallway to the staircase. Each prisoner was followed by his tormentor, jerked back if he walked too fast, pushed forward until he stumbled if he walked too slow. Bolt's neck was already sore. Could he survive this night? He concentrated on keeping his crutches out of the way of his guard's boots.

At the staircase the prisoners descended to the first floor. Bolt watched carefully and memorized the floor plan. It wasn't really that much different from the floor above. The containment center seemed to be right below the auditorium.

But that was where the similarities ended. First there was a long flight of steps taking them below the lowest level of the auditorium into a pit. The lighting revealed a dark gray haze in the air, almost a smoky look, but no smell. And when they reached the bottom of the pit, Bolt knew he had descended into hell. Long rows of tables paralleled hard benches, nothing like the cushy seats above them in the auditorium. Spaced along the hard benches, vertical poles rose to the invisible ceiling.

Groups of prisoners from other floors or areas of the building had already arrived in the containment center. Each prisoner sat by a pole, his hands uncuffed in front of him, but his neck tethered to the pole by his choke collar and chain. As Bolt's group was marched past the tables, he noticed the fear in the eyes of those chained to their pole.

Some were staring forward to the front of the room. Bolt turned his head. Oh, my. A bright gray light pierced the haze to illuminate an instrument of torture. It looked like a medieval rack. What had he gotten himself into?

By the time Bolt was chained to his pole and bench, his legs were feeling weak and he was breaking out in a cold sweat. At least Mr. Finkelstein was seated beside him, and both had their hands free. Would he be able to pass notes?

Looking around and seeing no guard within ear shot, Bolt leaned slightly toward Finkelstein. "Are you okay?" asked Bolt.

"Don't talk to me," whispered Mr. Finkelstein, looking straight ahead. "You'll get both of us placed on the stretcher."

"We want to help you," whispered Bolt, as he opened a book and pretended to be studying it. "Do you want to escape with us."

Magnified fear appeared in Finkelstein's eyes. "You fool. If they capture you, they will turn you into a zombie." He looked down at one of his books, and Bolt could see the beads of perspiration dotting his forehead.

"But—" began Bolt.

"I don't want to hear anymore," interrupted Finkelstein. "I am too old and slow. Besides, I have already sold my soul to Extor. Every time I fail to follow his orders, he jerks me back here for reeducation. He'll probably send me to the recycling center soon."

Finkelstein pulled a worn card from his pocket and pushed it to Bolt.

Bolt glanced at it as he slid it out of sight. Benecia again.

"So, The Palace of Light—" said Bolt.

"We're starting on page 137 in the red book," said Finkelstein, pointing at Bolt's books.

At that moment, a large hand slapped down on Bolt's shoulder from behind. "That's quite a bit of communication going on over here," said one of the guards. "Would the two of you like to be the first to try out the stretcher tonight?" His black glittering eyes peered out of his nebulous face and into Bolt's. Bolt put his head down.

"No, your honor," answered Mr. Finkelstein. "I was just telling the boy where we were with the classes."

"You would know," said the guard. "You seem to be here often. You realize, if you continue to disobey, we'll have to collect your free will plasma?" The guard walked off with a sinister chuckle.

"Find her," whispered Finkelstein. "She'll guide you...And if you succeed, please take care of my wife." He turned his back to Bolt.

Head between his hands, Bolt weighed the options. None were good. He flipped through the old books that sat in front of him. Maybe some previous prisoner had scribbled a hidden note that would provide some clues.

Clattering at the surrounding tables pulled him from his thoughts. Everyone was putting on headphones. Bolt placed his on and turned the dial to English. The lectures began.

Only tonight, the tone was different. No soft music and sales pitch, the instructor's tone was harsh and accusatory. He went into depth about the mistake of giving humans free will, and the research Extor was conducting to reverse this defect. And the source of the free will plasma for the research? Well, the failures of Extor's classes, of course. After all, if humans couldn't use their free will properly, especially after learning all the pleasures and rewards of a life lived by the principles of the night, why waste it? Why not put it to good use?

The lecturer continued, explaining that they had been selected and brought to the Strata, because they were thought to be good candidates to increase Extor's influence back in the surface world. But rebellious behavior would not be tolerated. This was basically their last chance. If they did not change their attitudes, they would be recycled.

He outlined the material they would cover this night and gave an overview of what they would hear when they returned to the auditorium.

By lunchtime, Bolt was struggling to stay awake. Leaning forward on the table would tighten the choke collar, as would falling asleep and leaning sideways. He pinched himself and kept his legs moving.

When they announced lunch, Bolt sat up straight. He thought there would be no food tonight. His stomach was growling. A wide screen at the front of the class came on, and a view of the auditorium above came into sharp focus, showing the visitors enjoying a delicious meal. Groans filled the containment center. Protests popped up throughout the group.

"Okay," barked the instructor. "So you don't want to watch your comrades eating?"

The screen went dark.

"How many of you would rather watch something else?" the instructor asked.

Finkelstein reached out and held Bolt's arm down. A few hands went up throughout the class.

"Now, would all of you who held up your hand, please stand?" continued the instructor.

A hush went through the containment center.

"Come, come, admit it," said the instructor. "We can play the video, if necessary, to see who you are."

A few frightened prisoners stood at their benches. The instructor turned on a video and found others who had raised their hands. Those unlucky few were unshackled from their poles, marched to the front of the class, and made to draw straws. Bolt became nauseous.

The prisoner with the short straw was an elderly white-haired lady. She stood straight with no tear in her eye, and glared at the instructor as he called four guards to the front of the room. A gasp went up from the seated prisoners.

The instructor paused. "Would someone else like to join us up front?"

The room fell deathly silent, and Finkelstein pushed down firmly on Bolt's shoulder to keep him from standing.

The guards then placed the unprotesting prisoner on the rack. And the others, who drew the long straws, were forced to turn the screws, in turns, at the instructor's command.

But the victim, stretched taut on the rack, refused to scream or beg for mercy. The instructor became more and more angry. The prisoners in the audience took their hands off their ears and sat transfixed. Who was this little lady? Where did she get this power? Finally, the instructor pushed away the prisoners who were turning the screws and began tightening the rack himself.

"You can torture and kill me," shouted the victim, "but you cannot take away my free will." Holding her head up and addressing those seated, she said, "Do not bend. Find the path of light."

Her face then filled with white light, as she turned to the instructor who was backing away from the rack. "By the power of Omni, I send you to your eventual destiny!"

A white explosion filled the room. The little lady disappeared, and a white ghost floated away from the rack. The bright light now shone on the place where the instructor had just stood. On the floor lay a pile of dark gray ashes.

Chapter Fourteen

Ghostly Chaos

The prisoners in the containment center gasped. Looking around, Bolt noticed that the light was not much brighter than before, but it was a lighter gray. The spotlight on the pile of ashes shone bright and white.

The wide screen at the front of the classroom flashed on. In big dark gray letters flashed the message, "CODE NIGHT, AUDITORIUM!" Immediately the large group of guards poured out of the classroom, locking the doors behind them.

Talking and commotion swept over the containment center. Prisoners stood and found that their chains were no longer tethered to their poles. Choke collars clattered on the tables as they were removed. Prisoners rushed to the doors and began trying to force them open. When they failed, the group dispersed and began looking for any other escape route.

Bolt stood and removed his choke collar. The ankle cuffs lay on the floor. Mr. Finkelstein sat, unmoving, head held in his hands.

"Aren't you going to look for an escape route?" asked Bolt.

"What good would it do?" responded Finkelstein. "You'll still be in The Palace of Night, and there will be hell to pay for all those who attempted escape."

Bolt started to sit down, then remembered the carts. "I'll be right back."

He surveyed the large classroom. Many doors opened off this area. The group of prisoners was moving from door to door, trying unsuccessfully to open them, then moving on to the next. How could he check all these rooms quickly? He picked the side of the room that would be under the laundry rooms, where there were four doors. The mob of prisoners had already checked them and moved on.

Bolt stood in front of the first door and faced the classroom. He slipped his wand from under his garment and held it behind his back. Pointing at the room behind him, he said, "*Hachthwilo!*[10]" He heard nothing. Would his wand even work down here? He moved to the second door and tried the same command. Again nothing. He tried again without success. He was never going to find the carts. He needed to get back to his seat before the guards returned.

At the fourth door he repeated, "*Hachthwilo!*" He heard a bump inside. Could it be? He moved directly in front of the knob. "*Tawenehil!*" He heard the lock click. Looking to see that no one was watching, he slipped into the dark room.

"*Wa'the'kilo,*" he whispered. A dim gray light came on. He heard footsteps outside the door and quickly turned the lock. The knob rattled. The footsteps moved away. Had someone seen him enter?

Turning to the room, he felt joy for the first time in two days. The carts sat huddled in a ring as if for protection. A quick inspection revealed no damage. But would they levitate in this environment? He climbed into his cart and turned on the levitator. It rose and spun. Yes! He set it down, and checked the others. They worked!

Now to get them out of here. There was only one door on the back side of the room. Was it possible? "*Tawenehilo!*" The lock clicked. He opened the door. A flight of stairs led to ground level. He hobbled outside the building, into the dim gray light.

Bursts of light gray filled the air like huge lightning bugs. Gray ghosts, shaped like puffy storm clouds, were swooping and darting. Then Bolt saw what the ghosts were chasing, huge black winged wolves. He rubbed his eyes. Yeah, they were still there. Was it safe to move the carts? He had to try.

He stood at the top of the steps, pointing his wand toward the carts. "*Piyalo!*[11]" The carts flew through the door and up the steps in single file, as if they were eager to escape. He counted windows and calculated where Room 362 was located. "*Hayalo!*[12]" He pointed his wand and guided the carts toward the roof over Room 362. A winged wolf swooped into the way. He put the carts into a dive and averted a collision. Finally the carts were over Room 362. He settled them onto the roof. "*Hapapilo!*[13]" They were ready.

Now he needed to get back to the classroom before the guards returned. He retraced his steps, closing and locking the exterior door. At the interior door, he stopped and listened. Footsteps again, and someone rattled the knob. Sounds of commotion continued in the classroom. Apparently the guards had not returned.

Bolt waited until the footsteps moved away, then slipped out and stood with his back to the door. Pointing his wand at the knob, he whispered, "*Shekwe*[14]." A thin

---

[10] Jump! (hahch-thwee-lo)

[11] Come! (pee-yah-lo)

[12] Go! (hah-yah-lo)

[13] Sit down! (hah-pah-pee-lo)

filament of goo flowed from his wand and filled the lock mechanism. He slipped his wand into his uniform and returned to the table.

Mr. Finkelstein remained head down, still shackled by his choke collar. He glanced briefly at Bolt, then back at the table.

"You're not going to try to escape?" asked Bolt.

Finkelstein didn't even look up. "They will be punished."

Bolt was thinking what he most needed to ask Finkelstein, when the wide screen at the front of the classroom came on again, showing a view of the auditorium above. Chaos filled the screen.

The prisoners in the containment center stopped their search for an escape route and gathered around the screen. Bolt stood so he could see better. Even Mr. Finkelstein looked up with interest.

The chaos was the same scene Bolt had witnessed outside. Black winged wolves darted through the air, chased by cloudy gray ghosts. Explosions and puffs of light gray light sparkled on the screen. Screams from the student prisoners drew Bolt's attention to the tables below, where the students were taking shelter. Where were the guards, the dark gray stratoids? Where was Extor?

Those in the containment center stood silently, like loyal fans watching their football team on the one yard line, and it was fourth down.

Suddenly, a massive explosion shook the room. The wide screen showed a bright flash of lightning at the exact instant a billboard-size opening appeared in the wall of the auditorium. The ceiling in the containment center continued to rattle, and the prisoners ducked for cover. Bolt's eyes remained riveted to the screen. The gang was in there.

Finally a stream of black winged wolves rocketed out the opening, followed by a mob of light gray ghosts. Static. And the wide screen went dark.

Bolt gazed at the blank screen. What had just happened? Worry about the gang made it hard to think about anything else. Had Extor and his stratoids just been attacked? Apparently the prisoners in the containment center thought so, because a loud cheer went up, and they rushed the door once again.

Before they could move a table to the door to use as a battering ram, a large gray ghost materialized at the front of the classroom, and again everyone became silent.

"Read the truth," said the ghost, in a booming voice that rattled the room. "Don't believe a word of what you are being told here."

He swung his arm like he was throwing a Frisbee, and a stack of papers flew through the air, depositing a pamphlet at each seat.

Then he walked to the storage room where the carts had been stored. "Poof," yelled the ghost, with a chuckle. A hole, six foot in diameter, appeared in the wall.

---

[14] Gum (shay-kway)

He repeated the process at the outside wall, and a hole and steps materialized. As he glided through the exit, he laughed and called to the prisoners, "Follow me if your dare, if you still have your free will."

And he was gone.

Half of the prisoners cautiously moved to the escape route, appearing uncertain whether they should attempt it. The rest moved back to their seats and began reading the pamphlet.

Bolt opened his pamphlet. This was a message from Contra, whoever that was, warning the prisoners of Extor to resist being brainwashed, explaining that Contra was the rightful coach for the influencers of darkness. Bolt flipped through the pamphlet, but found no map or explanation of Contra.

Mr Finkelstein sat silently beside him, head down, not touching the pamphlet.

"Aren't you going to read it?" asked Bolt.

"You don't want that on your desk when the guards come back," said Finkelstein.

"Has this happened before?" asked Bolt.

"Frequently," said Finkelstein. "And the guards will be back, either the old ones, or new ones that Extor has created."

What? Bolt's brain raced. He wanted that pamphlet. He snatched his pamphlet and Finkelsein's and stick-sprinted through the ghost exit. Standing outside the opening, a group of prisoners were milling around, not knowing where to go. Bolt slipped away from the group, pulled out his wand, and pointed at the pamphlets. "*Honthe'lo!*[15]" he whispered. The pamphlets flapped to the top of the building and dropped into the carts. Bolt hid his wand and reentered the classroom.

When he sat down once again, Finkelstein looked at him with a weak smile. "You certainly are a determined young man, first my fences and now the forces of evil." He hung his head and muttered, "You just might make it. Please take care of my wife."

"We're going to get you out of here, too," said Bolt.

Finkelstein just shook his head.

A quiet had settled on the classroom. Half of the students were reading their pamphlets, the other half had escaped. Bolt opened a pamphlet from the seat beside him and began reading in more detail.

The wide screen popped on and a strange stamping noise, like a printing press or a factory, filled the background. Extor appeared on the screen, so furious he was shaking. Yelling and waving his arms, he ordered the "visitors" back into their seats and instructed them to put on their headphones.

---

[15] Fly! (hon-they-lo)

"The danger is over," continued Extor. "We have vanquished the ghosts of Contra and sent them back to their cavern. Your guards will return momentarily. Anyone attempting escape will be punished severely. Pass those poisonous pamphlets down the table to the nearest aisle, and your guards will collect them. Anyone who keeps a pamphlet will pay dearly for such stupidity."

Finkelstein looked at Bolt with a questioning expression.

"I got rid of them," said Bolt.

Hypnotic music, like that played in the auditorium, filled the headphones. Two minutes later the entrance doors opened, and a small group of dark stratoids entered. One of them walked to the podium and announced that the agenda had been changed for the remainder of the day. They would be listening to the programming from the auditorium.

After about an hour of watching the screen intently for any views of damage to the auditorium, Bolt struggled to stay awake. Hunger gnawed at his stomach.

He was thinking of supper this morning, hoping he would get some, when the entrance doors opened again, and a larger group of dark guards entered. The leader announced that the rest of the day's classes would be canceled, and the prisoners would be returned to their rooms. Before that, however, they were instructed to put on their "reinforcer" pads.

As Bolt reached for his, he whispered to Finkelstein, "Grab a book and read, read, read. No other thoughts."

Finkelstein looked at him curiously, but reached for a book and opened it.

When the reinforcement session was over, the guards proceeded to cuff prisoners and fasten choke collars. Groups of prisoners were then marched out of the containment center, while half of the choke collars lay empty on the tables. Bolt followed Mr. Finkelstein back up the hall. Apparently the regular session in the auditorium had been canceled, also. Student prisoners packed the hallways, parting enough to let the chain gang through.

Back in his room, shackles and collar removed, Bolt stood, rubbing his sore neck and ankles. Where was the gang? He glanced out the window to the ground below. The group of containment center prisoners who had tried to escape had been rounded up. They were now being marched around the yard, tormented by guards with cattle prods. The fury in Bolt's chest began to rise again. He thought about using his wand to make the cattle prods explode, but that would only make the gang's escape more difficult.

He turned away, waiting for, hoping for, the return of Mad River Magic.

Chapter Fifteen

Preparations for Lift Off

*B*olt's stomach growled, his neck ached, and his anger boiled to the point he was ready to scream. Where was the gang? The hallway had been filled with "students" from the auditorium when he had been marched back from the containment center. The gang should have been back by now.

Terrible thoughts ran through his mind. What if the gang had been injured in the chaos and commotion of the ghost invasion? What if they had been moved somewhere else? Then the lock clicked, the door opened, and in walked Scout, Rey, Bug, and Lil. He had never been so happy to see them.

They rushed him and gave him a group hug.

"Where have you been?" asked Bolt, searching their faces.

They smiled proudly, like they were the winning team in a soccer match.

"We'll explain in a minute," said Rey. She checked the room for new bugs and set up blocking noise with the wands. The group moved to their conference area.

"We got it," whispered Bug.

"What, got what?" asked Bolt.

Rey silently pulled out an old book and handed it to Bolt. "This is what I was looking for, a history of the Strata."

Bolt leafed through the book, stopping at a map. Wow! "How did you get this?"

"I told you why I used the dark disguise," said Rey. "I had hoped to get a look at the professor's books while the groupies were asking him questions. I never got a chance."

"The ghost invasion?" asked Bolt.

"Yeah," said Rey. "How did you know about that?"

"They played it on the big screen in the containment center," he answered.

"Well, that changed my plans," she said. "After the early end to classes I thought there might be some chaos, especially with that hole blasted in the wall. So I sent Scout, Bug, and Lil to instigate trouble at the hole while I explored the podium. And voila!"

Bolt handed the book back to Rey. "Keep this hidden," he said. "We'll study and discuss it when we get out of here."

The gang beamed with their success. Lil and Bug gave each other a high five.

"So what did you learn today?" said Scout. "And when are we getting out of this gray hole?"

"Lots," said Bolt. "We'll discuss it today after supper. That should be in about an hour. I don't want to be in the middle of anything when the server shows up. Oh, I hope I get to eat, too."

The lock clicked, and the door opened. Rey hustled to hide the book, and everyone spread out. Bolt walked out into the common area to see what was going on.

The small stratoid meal server walked into the room pushing a cart with a single tray and quickly closed the door behind her. She put her finger to her lips, silencing Bolt, and quietly motioned him to take his seat at the table.

As she put his tray in front of him, she dropped a folded piece of paper and a business card on his lap. "I am instructed to inform you," she said, "that this empty tray is a reminder of the importance of assimilating the lessons you learn in the auditorium and the need to stay out of trouble."

She slid her short sleeve up her arm for an instant, revealing a white symbol with a cluster of flames. Then, touching his shoulder, she leaned forward and kissed him on the cheek. A light gray blush shone from her face, she spun, and disappeared out of the room.

What? Bolt felt color in his cheeks. He lifted the tray cover to find light gray food. He looked back at the door. All right! He was going to eat this before they discovered their mistake.

He slid the paper and card into his uniform and dug in. Never had strange gray food tasted so good. This wasn't what they served the rest of the prisoners. Had it been the server's meal?

As the growling in his stomach ceased, his curiosity grew. Quickly finishing the unidentified food, he moved back to his room and opened the paper. Another map of the Strata. And the same card Finkelstein had given him. Yes, it was time to make their move.

"What was that all about?" asked Rey, "pointing out to the table."

"Oh, just something the server was required to do as part of my punishment," said Bolt. Then whispering in her ear, "Don't say a word about her being here earlier, when she comes back with supper."

Rey looked at him with a question on her face, but nodded.

An hour later the server showed up again, this time with supper for the rest of the gang. With a gray blush on her cheeks, she apologized that she was not permitted to give him supper. She brushed her hand against his as she turned to leave the room. Bolt watched her walk out of the room, not sure what he was experiencing. She sure was pretty.

He found it difficult to get his mind off the server, but he willed himself to do so. They needed to make plans. He needed to bring the rest of the gang up to speed. It was time to act.

After the rest of the gang finished supper they all moved to their conference area. He updated them on Mr. Finkelstein, moving the carts to the roof, the pamphlets, Benecia's card, and the server's gray supper. He didn't mention the kiss. Yup, he had to stop thinking about that.

He ended with Finkelstein's advice or warning, "You'll never get out of here. You'll never be free."

The gang just looked at him with blank faces.

"So why are you so upbeat?" asked Rey. "It sounds like we should just crawl in a hole and die."

A tear formed in Lil's eye. Bolt had to turn this around. "Wait," he said. "I'm not saying we give up." He looked around the discouraged group. "I'm saying we have to get out of this place. And right now. With all the chaos of the ghost invasion, this is a good time." He lifted Lil's chin, slapped Scout on the shoulder, poked Bug until she slapped his hand. "We have a map, we have a contact, and we have the determination to succeed. Let's do it!"

"Yeah," said Bug. "We can do it."

The group huddled, put their hands together, and did their first Mad River Magic teamwork cheer. Bolt dared not say it, but the possibility of freedom was worth the risk of dying.

The group made their plans and set to work.

Scout modified the scavenged light beam into a welder/plasma cutter. He quickly zipped through the window bars and laid them aside carefully.

Bolt watched to see when the activity in the prison yard was farthest away, then called the carts down from the roof and in through the window. He and Scout began working on camouflaging the underbellies of the carts with gray sheets.

Chapter Sixteen

Code Gray, Laundry Room

*R*ey gathered the pamphlets and hid them away with the history book. She unlocked their door to the hallway with her "Tawenehilo" spell and looked at her "guest" uniform. They needed something else to wear, something that would blend in with the rest of the Strata. She was tired of wearing apples.

Rey stuck her head inside the door to the inner room where Bolt and Scout were preparing the barrel carts for their escape. "Bolt, we girls are going shopping," she said.

"What?" exclaimed Bolt. He looked at Rey like he didn't believe what he had just heard, or he thought she had finally lost it. The expression on his face was priceless. Why were boys so focused? Couldn't they ever see the big picture?

"We need some uniforms that will blend in better," said Rey. "We're going to turn in our dirty laundry and break into the laundry. There should be guard uniforms tucked away somewhere in there."

"I better go along with you," said Bolt.

"No, we can handle it," said Rey, pulling out her wand. "We're the three musketeers."

"Yeah," said Bug. "Don't get in our way." She waved her wand, in an imaginary sword fight.

"Well, don't take any chances," said Bolt. "If there is any hint of trouble, just come back. We can escape without new uniforms."

"But how long will we escape notice if we're wearing these prison apple grays?"

"Okay," said Bolt. "Be careful."

After looking down the hallway both ways, she saw that the coast was clear. The girls ran for the laundry room, pulling their dirty laundry bag behind them. They knocked on the door. No one answered.

Again checking that no one else was in the hallway, Rey held her wand behind her back and commanded, "*Tawenehilo!*" The lock clicked. The girls slipped inside and closed the door.

The light was on. Machinery was running from somewhere in the back or below.

"Let's look around," said Rey. "Lil, you keep watch on the hallway. Yell if someone is coming."

Shelves lined the walls and were filled with guest uniforms. There had to be something better. Bags of dirty laundry covered the floor, leaving only a path to the back.

Rey and Bug looked through the shelves of clean laundry. Nothing but prison apple gray. Ugh.

They moved to the back where a door led into a smaller dark room. No uniforms. But a light shone from a staircase leading down to the second level. The machinery sounded like it was coming from that level. Rey motioned Bug to follow her, and tiptoed down the steps.

The bottom of the steps opened into a large room with bright lights and loud noise. Probably a washer. She'd never heard anything quite like that before. Rey peeked around the corner, but saw no stratoids. They moved cautiously into the front room. Still no one. But the shelves contained a variety of guard uniforms.

Rey and Bug sorted through the uniforms and picked out five that looked similar to the uniform worn by their meal server. They were heading back to the staircase when they heard the lock on the hall door click.

The girls took the steps two at a time as they hurried back to Lil.

"Quick, let's get out of here," Rey whispered.

But the door to the hallway was stuck and wouldn't budge. They heard footsteps coming up the steps.

Rey motioned for Bug and Lil to hide under the laundry bags. The three girls had no sooner slid under the bags, when the footsteps entered their room. They held their breath. Whoever was present in the room said nothing. The footsteps paused for a few seconds, then returned to the stairway, turning off the gray light on the way out.

Rey, Bug, and Lil waited until they heard no activity below. They crawled out from under the stinky laundry bags and tried the lock again. Still jammed. With all three wands pointed at the lock in unison, they managed to melt the whole lock set.

"Well, I guess they'll know someone broke in," said Rey. "Let's get back to the room."

"Wait," said Bug. "Why don't we open the back door to make it look like someone escaped in that direction?"

Bug opened the door just a crack, then the girls hurried out the door and into the hall. As Rey closed the door, she thought she saw a gray blur slide back into the back room.

"Come on," whispered Rey. "Hurry."

The three musketeers ran down the hallway and slid into their room. Huffing and puffing, they showed Bolt and Scout their new escape attire, and told them about their near miss.

"I think it's time to make our move," said Bolt. "We have the barrel carts ready."

After quickly changing into the server uniforms the gang hopped into their carts. While Bolt was checking outside the window, the alarm went off.

"Code gray, third floor laundry," announced the mechanical voice from the wall speaker.

Bolt took one more look out the window. "Good, while they're focused on the laundry room, we'll slip out in the other direction."

As he climbed into his cart and the gang turned on their levitators, the lock on the hall door clicked and the door opened.

Mad River Magic flew out the window, while a voice behind them yelled, "Stop!"

Bolt led them up and over the top of the building. Here they wouldn't be visible from the inside of the visitor center. The sound of alarms and yelling from the ground below told the gang that they had better move out quickly.

Chapter Seventeen

From Gauntlet to Flying Wolves

*B*olt kept the carts close to the roof of the visitor center. He didn't want the guards to see them. They were probably surrounding the building by now. So, which direction to go? He had studied the map in Rey's book, and he knew which direction to take toward Solia's palace of light. But the set where Benecia worked was in the opposite direction. And that would take them directly over all the activity at the laundry room. Could he find a way to circle around?

He spun his cart to survey the surroundings. The visitor center sprawled like an octopus with arms stretching out in many directions. They had seen only one wing.

He looked up. Unlike other areas of the Strata, no visible ceiling confined their vertical movement. In fact, looking into the distance he could see vertical walls rising like sky scrapers with connections to layer after layer of The Strata.

But one thing that hadn't changed, this whole world radiated a dim gray light. Gray light and plastic layers, how suffocating. Oh, they had to get out of here.

Bolt decided on a path that would take them in the wrong direction, back to the hub of the building. From there they would follow the roof of another wing leading in approximately the right direction, but keeping them away from the laundry room. Mad River Magic zipped along, close to the shiny gray roof, watching for trouble.

They dodged around a huge cage of ugly winged wolves. Bolt wanted to rain fire on the monsters, but he didn't want to tip off the guards as to their location. He did melt the lock on their door into a solid mass of metal. Hopefully that would keep them in their cage longer. Something told him that he should take more drastic measures, but there was no time.

They reached the hub, where they turned back toward their original destination. No guards had appeared to chase them...yet.

And then Mad River Magic saw them. Blast! He knew they would show up. Gray guards were popping up along the roof like guard towers surrounding a prison. Blast, it was never easy.

As each tower sprang into place, an open platform appeared at the top. And on the platform, manned by a dark gray guard, a swiveling cannon began spraying a laser-focused beam of black light. The black beams criss-crossed the top of the building and the space above them, searching for their target.

Bolt remembered their experience with the cage truck and the effect of that light. He didn't want that again. Where could they hide?

He looked up again. Now that the gang had been discovered, there was no point in staying close to the roof. They had open space above them. There wasn't any place to hide on the roof. They didn't have a choice.

Okay, let's do it! Bolt led the gang in a steep climb away from the guards, but the guards saw them and began zapping them with their black light cannons. After two near crashes for Lil and Bug, Bolt knew that their strategy wasn't going to work.

He instructed Rey and the rest of the gang to create a smoke screen high above the action, and stay put. At least the guards wouldn't be able to see them. Then he dived back into the action below. Swooping low into the courtyard between the two lines of guards, he entered the gauntlet. Zipping back and forth, and up and down, he dodged the black lights. While the guards tried to hit him, he dropped and climbed, backtracked with vertical loops, and shot ahead.

Now, move up a little higher. Looking at both sides, he adjusted the height of his cart. Perfect.

The guards were so intent on destroying Bolt, that they didn't notice he was now directly between the two wings of the building, and the guards were directly in the line of fire. When the black lights were pointed at Bolt, they were also aimed at the guards on the adjacent wing. The guards were unknowingly zapping each other.

"Yeah, guys. Catch me if you can." Bolt zigged and zagged as he raced for the finish line.

Rey, seeing what was happening below and the fun the rest of the gang was missing, divided the group in half. She and Lil took the left flank. Scout and Bug took the right flank. While the gray guards were focused on Bolt, Mad River Magic swept along the wings behind the guards. Any guards who had survived the black lights from the opposite wing were targeted.

Rey zipped in from behind with her wand ready. "*Chaki tekhaaka!*[16]" she yelled as she passed each guard. The black light exploded in a cloud of dust that engulfed the

---

[16] small ax, tomahawk (chak-kee tayk-haah-kay)

guard. The guard tower collapsed, and both the light and the guard disappeared into a pile of dark gray smoke. Scout and Bug used the same spell on their side of the courtyard, hop-scotching down the wing, taking out any black lights and guards that had not already been zapped from the opposite side.

When the gang had completed their counterattack, Bolt came out of the gauntlet unscathed except for a few scorch marks on his cart. They had systematically destroyed the line of black light cannons on two wings of Extor's palace.

Mad River Magic yelled and gave high fives. Yes! They could do this. Now let's get out of here before any more goons show up.

Bolt glanced at his card and map. Layer 2018 was the strata they were looking for. He turned his cart into a steep climb. The quicker they were tiny specks in this pit, and high above the visitor center, the better. Bolt glanced back to see if the rest of the gang was keeping up with him, and that's when he saw their next challenge.

Flying cage trucks, five of them. Blast.

"You guys stay together," called Bolt. "And keep heading for Layer 2018." He pulled the sheet off the bottom of his cart. It was of no use now for camouflage, and it was slowing him down. He leaned out of his cart and pulled the sheets off the bottom of the other carts.

Bolt banked out of formation and set a course directly toward the cage trucks. They were closing fast. He saw a red blur to his right. Bug. No.

"Go back," he shouted.

"No." Bug clenched her jaw. "I can fly as well as you. We're in this together. So what's the strategy?"

Bolt handed her two sheets. "Paste these to their windshields."

She nodded.

They were seconds from contact. Bolt picked the lead truck and buzzed over the cab, missing by inches. "*Tehashichtheto!*[17]" he commanded, as he pointed his wand at the windshield. A thin layer of adhesive covered the windshield. He turned a tight vertical loop and spread a sheet over the paste.

He turned to Bug, who was laughing and giving him two thumbs up. Not to be outdone, she did a horizontal swipe over two of the trucks at once, plastering their windshields, splat, splat. Another loop and she lay down the two sheets. She finished with her hand held as an imaginary gun, blowing the smoke from the muzzle.

Bolt shook his head and grinned, then covered the two remaining trucks with side by side vertical loops, laying down the paste on the first pass, then spreading the sheets.

---

[17] Paste! (tay-hah-sheech-thay-to)

Now Bolt and Bug danced in front of the trucks, zig-zagging back and forth. They stayed just a few feet in front of them, egging them on. Bug looked ahead, then nodded to Bolt. She understood the strategy.

With one second to impact into the vertical wall at the perimeter of the pit, Bolt and Bug shot straight up. Blinded by dirty windshields, the five cage trucks plowed straight into the wall, crumbling into a mass of plastic and metal. Bolt looked back to watch the junk slide down the wall to the bottom of the pit.

After a high five, Bolt and Bug zipped back to the rest of the gang at full speed. Scout, Rey, and Lil, stood at the edge of Layer 2018, clapping and cheering. Bug jumped out of her cart and took a bow.

Bolt smiled and felt satisfaction in knowing they were out of the pit. Certainly there were bigger challenges ahead, and the risk was...he didn't want to think about it. But they were a team, and they were setting their own destiny.

Now let's find Benecia.

"Come on gang," said Bolt, "let's get out of here before any more Extor posses show up." He showed everyone the map. "This is the stage or set we're looking for, Benecia's stage."

Bolt led them high against the ceiling of Layer 2018, but he kept looking back. What would Extor send next?

Soon they were over the edge of Strata buildings. The brighter light of daytime sleeping hours was fading, and stratoid activity was picking up. Wow, they sure could use those sheets for camouflage now. Bolt looked around and spotted a tank for liquid of some sort. The gang set down and investigated. No stratoids around. Bolt sniffed the liquid. No smell. He dared not stick his finger into it.

Scout pulled a tube out of his pocket and dipped it into the liquid. He attached his wand to the end of the tube. "*Tepika!*[18]" he commanded.

A buzzing sound emanated from the wand. After two seconds, a mechanical voice announced, "H_2O, with trace unidentified minerals."

Scout turned to the gang. "Water."

Bolt watched with amusement. What a crew.

They smeared the bottoms of their carts with the water, then threw on dust, covering the paint. Bolt waved his wand, "Let there be gray."

And they were off again. In spite of the humor, everyone seemed to be on edge, looking back repeatedly. Hopefully Benecia was working today, and they could find her before any more of Extor's cronies identified them.

Finally, after skirting multiple sets, Bolt was satisfied that they had found Benecia's set. He double-checked his map, and the gang set their carts down behind

---

[18] Measure! (tay-pee-kah)

a shed on the perimeter. They checked each other to make certain no color was showing, and set off for the center of activity.

A large empty stage stood in the middle of two groups of stratoids, dark gray on one side and light gray on the other. They peered through binocular-like devices, and called instructions. But who were they directing? Bolt couldn't see anyone on stage. Cheers would come from one side, moans from the other. Strange.

The gang spread out and made their way to the light gray side. A pair of the vision devices lay unused on a table. Bolt picked them up and looked toward the stage. He almost dropped them. There on the stage were two men standing on a sidewalk. It looked like the World Trade Center in the distant background. One of the men was pleading for mercy, the other appeared ready to deliver retribution.

"Kill him," yelled the dark gray stratoids.

"No, have mercy." Pleaded the light gray stratoids.

The pleading man had tears in his eyes. The other punched him. He went down.

The dark gray directors cheered. "Finish him off."

"Stop," yelled the light gray stratoids. "Give him another chance."

Bolt was mesmerized. With the device down he saw or heard nothing but the opposing stratoids. With the device up, he saw and heard all of the tension of the actors on the stage...or was it really a stage? How could this be?

He was putting the device to his eyes again when he felt a tap on his shoulder.

"Can I help you?" It was one of the light gray directors. He had a curious smile on his face. "You must be new around here."

"Yes, I'm sorry," said Bolt. "I'm looking for Benecia."

"Ah, of course," said the stratoid. He pointed to a stratoid sitting on a director's chair at the back of the light-gray group.

"Thanks," said Bolt.

"Welcome to our set," answered the stratoid. "Good luck with your new job."

"Thank you," said Bolt. Wow, this friendliness was new.

He gathered the gang, and they approached Benecia. A tall slender stratoid with white hair, she was watching the action on the set. She looked up as the gang approached. Her large off-white cape sported a pure white flame symbol on the front. She was the lightest stratoid Bolt had seen thus far.

Bolt showed her the card he had been given by the server at the visitor center. He had just finished introductions, when all the stratoids around the set began buzzing and pointing at the ceiling.

Turning to see what they were pointing at, Bolt's heart sank. A pack of flying wolves approached at amazing speed. Blast, why hadn't he fried that cage back at the visitor center?

He looked around the set for a hiding place, then turned to Benecia.

"Come with me," she said, jumping out of her chair. She moved with agility and speed, her director's cape flowing behind her. Mad River Magic ran to keep up.

Looking over his shoulder, Bolt saw that they had only seconds until the wolves would arrive. They dodged around a large building, out of sight from the wolves. A hole in the floor of the Strata stopped them.

"Get in," said Benecia. The fear in her voice told Bolt they had no option.

The gang jumped in, and Benecia spread her cape over the hole, hiding them from view.

Under the cape, the gang looked terrified. They knew the consequences of capture and return to the visitor's center.

Bolt pulled them into a huddle. "Benecia knows what she's doing," he whispered.

Above the cape, the noise of wolf howls and large flapping wings settled onto the set. Yelling and arguing from the influencers filled the air. "They went that way," called one side. "No they went over there," yelled the other.

The scratching of wolves' feet on the floor of the strata came closer. Low wheezing howls moved in around the hole. Bolt felt the gang trembling. They were surrounded. There was no way out.

"Stop!" yelled Benecia. "You have no right to invade my space. Now get out of here and return to The Palace of Night."

"We have orders from Extor," wheezed a low-pitched voice, "to capture and return the prisoners. Now get out of our way."

A scuffle began above them, then a large dark gray jaw bit into the cape and whisked it away from the hole.

Bolt and the gang looked up to see the wolves surrounding them. Snarling and wheezing and howling, they began to open and close their huge reptilian wings, while bared teeth revealed massive canines.

"Climb out one at a time," wheezed the apparent leader of the pack, "or we will snap your necks." His attempted chuckle ended in a cough.

Behind and above the wolves, Benecia stood on the roof of a nearby building, holding a large wand with a crystal tip. As she swirled it in circular manner, a laser-sharp beam of gray light flowed from the wand into the eyes of the wolves. The wolves froze and became silent.

Another beam of white light dropped like a rope into the center of the hole.

"Climb out one at a time," called Benecia. "Look up at me. Do not look at the wolves."

The gang looked at Bolt with uncertainty. He stepped forward and grasped the white light. A velvet-soft touch met his hand. He tested the strength with a pull. The light didn't budge. He hung with all his weight. It held him. He hooked his crutches to his pants, and hand over hand, climbed out of the hole, keeping his eyes on

Benecia. When he reached her roof, she grasped his hand and swung him effortlessly to her side.

The rest of the gang followed. When all were on the roof, Benecia handed off the gray light to one of her assistants, who continued the hypnotic motion into the wolves' eyes. The beam of white light then bristled with tongues of fire as Benecia aimed it at the wolves' wings. One at a time a sizzle and plume of dark gray smoke rose from the ring as the light moved around the circle. When Benecia was finished, the wolves were fused together in a solid ring.

"Follow me," said Benecia, as she hurried down a ladder and stepped into a floating box.

Mad River Magic climbed into Benecia's transportation, and it shot off toward a cluster of buildings in the distance. Rey leaned out of the back and aimed her wand at the hidden barrel carts. "*Neekata!*[19]" she called. And the barrel carts lined up behind Benecia's box in single file.

"We must hurry," said Benecia. "We have little time before reinforcements arrive."

---

[19] Follow! (naay-kah-tah)

Chapter Eighteen

Benecia and the Gray Bird

*B*enecia stopped the floating box in front of a small square building with windows, then led the way through the front door.

"Put your carts in that room." She pointed at a room with a table and a single chair.

Bolt aimed his wand at the carts. "*Piyalo!*" he commanded. The carts filed into the eating room.

Bolt looked around Benecia's house. A staircase led to a second level and presumably Benecia's sleeping room. Turning around in the small space, he saw that three rooms made up the first level, the eating room, a living room, and a food preparation room.

Benecia hurried them into the living room. "Listen carefully," she said. "I must speak quickly. I fear we will have unwanted guests very soon. I know that your goal is to reach The Palace of Light. There you must speak to Solia. Don't let anyone prevent you from speaking to her. Your journey will be dangerous and filled with challenges, but if you follow my instructions, you will succeed."

She handed each of the gang a large crystal. "Put these on the tips of your wands. They will give you additional power from Solia. The light from the white crystal has the power to shine light on the evil and immobilize your enemy. And you will encounter many."

"But how do we get to the Palace of Light?" asked Bolt. "Is there any way to return to our world without going first to the Palace of Light?" There had to be a quicker way.

"Only Omni has the power to safely return people from the Strata to your world," said Benecia. "Extor has risen from the depths of darkness and stolen the position of dark-gray influencer from Solia's brother, Contra. And Extor has somehow found a way to create apertures into your world, using the visitor's center as part of his scheme to gain increased influence for the dark side. You can't get through Extor's apertures without protection from Omni."

"Then who is Omni?" asked Bolt. "How do we find him?" This seemed so complicated.

"Omni is the ultimate power of the Strata," said Benecia. "But you need Solia to reach Omni."

Rey groaned. A tear formed in Lil's eye. Scout looked down and shuffled his feet.

"Come on, gang," said Bolt. "We can do this. We've worked together so far." He turned to Benecia. "So tell us how to get to Solia and The Palace of Light."

Benecia hurried to the window and peeked around the curtain. She returned to the gang. "We must hurry. They will be here soon."

She handed each member of the gang a white ticket. "These are tickets for the white bird that flies to The Palace of Light. When you leave here, you will find yourself in a history shaft. Follow my instructions carefully. You will fly back to Strata 333. There you will see a sign for the lightport, and at the lightport you will see the big white bird. Take the white bird to The Palace of Light, and don't get off anyplace between here and there. Beware the Desert of Indecision, the Hemlock Forest, and the poison water. If you are attacked, use your crystal wand to paralyze the enemy."

Benecia paced the floor, checking the window repeatedly.

"Now get your carts lined up at the bottom of the steps and..." Benecia rushed to the window. "It's here!"

She rushed back to the gang and gave each of them a hug. "Get your carts lined up and get in. When I go out the front door, Bolt, you count to ten, then hit the bottom of the banister."

"But what about you?" cried Lil.

Benecia squeezed her hand. "I will be okay. Now move."

As Benecia stepped out the door, Bolt began counting. He heard a faint buzz coming from the front yard. He could hear Benecia yelling at someone or something. A dust-like haze began seeping in around the windows. A feeling of lethargy and indecision crept into his mind. Did they really want to do this? Maybe they should wait until tomorrow.

"Bolt, now!" The sound of Benecia's yelling brought him to his senses.

He hit the banister. A rumble filled the house as the upstairs ceiling and the roof slid back. A power like he had never felt before quivered inside his cart. And then his cart blasted off like a rocket, up the staircase and through the roof. A sharp turn put him upside down against the ceiling of the strata.

He looked back to see the gang following him, Scout hanging tightly to his controls, Bug raising her arms like she was riding a roller coaster. Rey and Lil had determined faces. Yes, they were beginning the journey home.

As they rolled back to upright and zipped farther and farther away, Bolt looked back to see a cloud of dust surrounding Benecia's house. Even from their distance, he could hear the deafening roar like a cloud of locusts. An invisible wall held back the swarm, as Benecia waved her white light up and down.

Bolt motioned for the gang to give the carts full power. They shot forward and instantly were in a history shaft speeding down. The numbers whizzed past them. When they hit strata 1000, Bolt motioned for the gang to slow down. 900, 800, 700. They saw a sign that said "Exit next stop for LightPort." Hmm, Bolt thought Benecia said Strata 333, but then there was so much chaos going on. Bolt took the exit. The gang followed.

The gang gathered around the exit sign, 666.

"Why did you get off here?" asked Rey. "I thought she said Strata 333."

"She did," said Bolt. "But see the sign." He pointed. "It says LightPort. Let's check it out." Full of apprehension, the gang looked around as they followed the signs. But, indeed, they found the LightPort, and there perched the white bird.

As they handed the attendant their tickets and checked their carts, Bolt noticed that no one else was in line to get on the flight. When they stepped into the plane, Rey looked around as if she was skeptical. The interior was definitely light gray, not white.

Bolt and Rey looked at each other. She was probably thinking the same thing he was. Should they get off? But the doors closed, and the flight attendant announced their destination as The Palace of Light. Leaning back and thinking of all the things Benecia had told them, Bolt still couldn't relax.

The white bird flapped down the runway and slowly picked up speed. Then, with wings spread wide, she accelerated and soared into the sky. Bolt noticed that they were over the pit of the visitor's center and quickly followed a shaft that took them out over a desert. Ah, the Desert of Indecision.

Bolt turned to Rey and gave her a thumbs up. She didn't look so convinced.

Looking out the window again, Bolt saw the lighter daytime hours were approaching. And as the surroundings became lighter, the white bird was becoming a gray bird.

He began to inspect the interior of the white bird. It was changing, too. Faint cross hatched lines showed up in the background of the entire cabin. The seats were definitely gray now. Even the cabin seemed to be shrinking. He looked out the window. In the lighter hours of daytime, the bird was clearly not white. His heart sank.

Bolt looked at Rey. She looked increasingly anxious. Her facial expression said, "What do we do?"

He got out of his seat and approached the flight attendant. She stood to face him. She was now gray and dressed in a guard uniform.

"Return to your seat," she said, "and don't get up until we land."

"Is this bird going to The Palace of Light?" asked Bolt.

No longer smiling, a sneer covered her gray face. "I think you know the answer to that question. Now get back to your seat."

Bolt moved slowly back to his seat, his mind racing as he looked for an escape route. The attendant was at the front of the cabin. An emergency escape door was near their seats, but the bird was flying higher than the carts had ever flown. And the carts were stored in the luggage compartment below them.

Bolt slid into the seat beside Scout. They huddled, and Scout nodded his head. Bolt then motioned Rey, Lil, and Bug to join him in the row in front of Scout, who opened his bag, then crouched behind his seat. As the rest of the gang kept up a steady stream of chatter, Bolt aimed his wand over his shoulder.

"*Mshikanwi!*[20]" he commanded. A steady stream of air flowed over his shoulder to dissipate any fumes.

Bolt looked out the window. They were landing, and he didn't see any white palace. In fact, as they hit a dark gray runway, he saw a cage truck waiting at the far end. He whispered instructions to the rest of the gang.

As the big gray bird slowed on the runway, Bolt approached the attendant guard. "Why are we not going to the Palace of Light?" He moved beside her to direct her attention away from the gang.

"You fool," snarled the guard. "Do you think you can escape Extor? Once he catches you in his aperture, you belong to him forever. Now get back in your seat."

Bolt shoved her backward into the bathroom. Then, pointing his wand at the lock, commanded "*Shekwe!*" A filament of thick, sticky, resin filled the lock. He did the same with the lock to the cockpit, then hobbled quickly back to the gang. They had already dropped through the hole in the floor and were waiting in the luggage compartment below.

Bolt dropped his crutches into the opening and lowered himself through Scout's hole, joining the rest of Mad River Magic. "Get into your carts and be ready for take-off."

Holding his wand at ready, Bolt waited for the plane to stop. When the plane lurched, he pointed at the cargo door. "*Kekilshimthoothwa!*[21]" he commanded. An invisible bison blasted the door open, and the gang rocketed out, following Bolt.

---

[20] Wind! (mshee-kah-nwee)

He glanced at his map and got the gang into formation, heading toward the Palace of Light. Looking back, as expected, he saw the cage truck was on their tail.

"Keep going toward that spot of light," said Bolt to Rey, pointing off into the distance. "I'm going to fix that truck permanently." He peeled out of formation.

Expecting Bug to join him, he was surprised when Lil pulled up on his right flank.

"It's my turn to have some fun," said Lil. "You and Bug have been doing all the magic."

"Okay," said Bolt, looking at Bug who had arrived on his left side. "Try out your crystal light to immobilize them while Lil does her thing."

Bug pointed at the truck with a white laser emanating from her crystal.

"Okay, Lil," said Bolt, "what do you have in mind?"

"Watch this." She flew over the truck and waved her wand. Five miniature flying carts appeared in front of the truck. She returned to Bug and Bolt.

"Now turn off the light," said Lil.

Bug turned off the white laser. Lil pointed her wand at the miniature carts and directed them to curve off to the side. The truck followed. The gang cheered.

"We're not done yet," said Lil, smiling deviously.

The carts turned a full one hundred eighty degrees and headed back to the airport. The gang held their breath as the truck followed. Bolt grinned. What was her target? The truck got closer and closer to the airport. The miniature carts splatted into the control tower antennas, and the cage truck followed. It took out the entire communication capabilities of the airport as it skimmed the control tower then crashed on the airport terminal roof.

Mad River Magic clapped, while Lil stood in her cart and took a bow.

"Well done, Lil," said Bolt, as they headed off toward their point of light and their destination. "Hopefully that will keep them occupied for awhile." But somehow he knew Extor had other unlimited options, and their battles were just beginning.

The airport surroundings quickly gave way to an empty desert. Low sand dunes swirled and eddy currents kicked up gray, dusty cyclones. Littering the floor below, abandoned vehicles of all types lay partially buried in the gray sand. But no human or stratoid inhabitants were to be seen.

Remembering the cloud of dust back at Benecia's house and the effect it had on him, Bolt carefully dodged the gray tornadoes. The map had labeled this as the Desert of Indecision. He wasn't about to lose his determination.

Soon, they were over small scrub-like growth that resembled miniature trees. Something about them looked familiar. The trees became larger and larger as the gang moved toward the Palace of Light. Flecks of light gray and dark gray sparkled

---

[21] Buffalo bull (kay-keel-shee-m-thoo-thwah)

from their branches. Then it hit Bolt. Yes, the hemlock tree sitting back in Cedar Heights at the aperture to the Strata. Man, he wished there was an aperture at this end that would take them back home.

When the trees began to look like full-sized specimens, Mad River Magic crossed a river and was suddenly over the edge of the forest. A road appeared below them, and then their carts lost power. They managed to land on the road before their turbo-levitators died completely.

"What now?" asked Rey. She was looking around frantically as she held tightly to her cart.

Bug walked toward the river. "I'm thirsty," she said.

"Don't touch that water," yelled Bolt. "That's the Hemlock River, and it's poisonous. Remember what Benecia said?"

"It looks crystal clear," said Bug. "Just a little sip shouldn't hurt. We haven't had anything to drink for hours."

"Don't be stupid, Bug," said Scout. "Poison can be completely invisible." He walked over to the river and pulled out his tube analyzer. Using a piece of gray grass and being careful to not touch the water with his hand, he dipped the grass into the river. Holding his analyzer over the wet grass, he waited a second, then whistled. "Wow, coniine, 100 milligrams per ounce. That's the poison in wild hemlock, and one ounce of that water is enough to kill you." He shook his head and carefully dropped the wet grass, which had curiously turned black.

"Come on," said Bolt. "Let's follow this road. The sooner we get to the Palace of Light, the sooner we can have something to eat and drink."

The carts wouldn't fly. But as Scout tinkered with his, he discovered that they would drive. Mad River Magic proceeded into the Hemlock Forest, following the road. It was leading in the right direction.

Frustrated with their slow progress, Bolt looked around. Through the trees, the desert was still visible. Wind whipped eddy currents that died at the edge of the forest. Which was better, the protection of the forest, or the speed they could achieve flying? It was a tough decision. Wow, he wished he could ask someone else for advice.

Rey was carefully studying her map. The road and the forest gradually became darker. As he looked more carefully at the trees, he noticed the needles were turning darker gray as the night time hours moved closer.

A road sign appeared ahead. The gang stopped to study it. "Solia's Palace of Light, 60 miles." And below it was a dark gray sign, "Road Closed ahead. Turn back before it is too late."

Lil and Bug turned to Bolt, questions in their faces, fear starting to creep in at the edges.

"What now?" asked Rey.

"I'm not surprised," said Bolt. "I would be willing to bet that we'll see many more obstacles ahead. But remember, Benecia told us we could succeed." He pulled the gang into a huddle. "We just have to believe and stick together."

"I have an idea," he said. "I can still see the edge of the desert over there." He pointed through the trees. "Maybe if we can get to the desert, our turbos will work again."

"Yeah!" yelled Bug. She slapped the side of her barrel cart. "Let's do it. Let's get these things flying."

Scout didn't look so brave, but he smiled a worried smile and nodded.

Rey and Lil agreed after some discussion.

Mad River Magic turned their carts into the forest and headed for the desert, avoiding each hemlock tree by as much distance as possible. The ground was rough. They had to get out and push their carts at some spots. And if the pushing was not difficult enough, the hemlock needles under their feet burned and prickled like touching an electric fence.

Bolt wiped the perspiration off his brow. This better work, or the gang wasn't going to be too happy with him.

After pushing and pulling their carts for nearly an hour, they finally reached the desert. Bolt and Scout dragged their carts out into the fine gray sand first, while the girls watched. A feeling of lethargy was quickly overcoming Bolt. He brushed the sand off his clothes and hopped into his cart. It flew!

"Brush off all the sand before you get into your cart," Bolt yelled at Scout.

Scout's cart worked, too.

Soon the whole gang was back in business, zipping over the desert at full speed, heading for that dot of light sixty miles in the distance.

As the dark hours became darker, it became more difficult to dodge the little tornadoes of gray sand that swirled up into the air. The gang flew higher. Yet even at that altitude they occasionally hit eddy currents.

Looking down at the desert, Bolt was certain he could see little cloud-shaped monsters with puffed cheeks blowing ever harder, creating ever bigger sand tornadoes to trap them. And when he looked up, he was caught in one. The current sucked their carts into a funnel and spun them round and round until they were covered with the hypnotic dust. It then dumped them on top of a gray dune.

Mad River Magic climbed out of their carts. But instead of frantically looking for escape, they yawned and sat in the sand.

"Let's take a break," said Rey. "I'm really tired."

Even Bug yawned and stretched. And soon they were all asleep on the sand.

Chapter Nineteen

Contra and the White Castle

*A*fter an unknown length of time, Bolt woke to the banging of metal. He sat up and looked around. Where was he? Oh, yeah, the Desert of Indecision.

Gray ghosts, like those he had seen in the containment center, were tapping and messing with their barrel carts. They rolled and tumbled, changing shape as they explored the carts. Bolt jumped up.

"What are you doing with our carts?" he demanded of one of the ghosts.

The largest of the ghosts floated to the front. "So you have fallen prey to the magic sleeping dust?" He laughed and spun around. "We were inspecting your contraptions to see how they work. What do they do?"

"Who are you?" asked Bolt.

"I am Contra," said the ghost in a loud booming voice. "And I see you have taken the advice I gave you when you were in the containment center."

"How did you know that I was in the containment center?" asked Bolt.

Contra laughed and held up one of the pamphlets that he had found in the carts. "I'm glad someone is reading what I have taken so much time and effort to write and distribute. I'm guessing that you are on your way to Solia's Palace of Light."

Bolt nodded, not knowing what to say to an obviously powerful being.

"Why is it that all humans who escape Extor try to reach Solia's Palace of Light rather than my cavern?" asked Contra, chuckling as if he already knew the answer.

"I appreciate the pamphlet and your advice," said Bolt. "Can you help us get to the Palace of Light, safely?"

Contra rubbed his nebulous face with his hand, deep in thought. "I never do favors for my holier-than-thou sister, but maybe we can make a deal. If you will show me how these contraptions might help me fight Extor, and promise to someday help me defeat him, I will take you to my sister's gate."

Bolt thought carefully. He didn't have a choice. What was he getting himself into now? "I will show you how these carts work, if you will agree to take me to Solia. Deal?"

"Show me," answered Contra.

By now the rest of the gang was awake and was standing behind Bolt.

Bolt turned to the gang. "Keep your wands hidden and follow me." He led the gang to their carts. "We'll do a vertical loop in single file, then each of us will snare a ghost with Rey's 'kchiptilo' spell. And remember, keep your wand hidden in your hands, and do not let them see it."

The gang nodded, and they were off. First they buzzed the ghost group, then they did a large vertical loop, each member pulling out to snare a ghost. "*Kchiptilo, kchiptilo, kchiptilo, kchiptilo, kchiptilo,*" as light seemed to erupt from the steering wheel of each cart. The five ghosts standing closest to Contra were now harnessed in a fiberglass vest. And a leash from each vest was tethered to a large glass rod erupting from the sand.

The gang set their carts down, and Bolt approached Contra.

"Good enough?" asked Bolt.

Contra inspected the harnesses wrapped tightly around his companions. "I'm not impressed," he said, as he continued to look back and forth between the carts and the harnesses. "But I will take you to my sister. Let her know that I saved you."

"I will." Bolt breathed a sigh of relief. Finally they were making progress. Oh, he hoped that Solia would have an answer.

Contra climbed into Bolt's cart. "I will fly your cart to my sister's palace. You can ride with one of your buddies."

Bolt climbed onto the back of Scout's cart, holding his crutches. "You think this cart can handle both of us?" he asked.

Scout looked apprehensively at Bolt, but didn't say anything. He appeared to be more worried about Contra's ghosts that were floating around the gang, looking into their carts.

"Come on," Bolt called to Rey, Bug, and Lil, "get in your carts and let's get going."

The girls climbed in, and Mad River Magic lifted off. Contra fumbled with the controls to Bolt's cart, but finally got the cart flying. They headed out across the Desert of Indecision, Mad River Magic and Contra surrounded on all sides by the ghosts.

The lighter hours were arriving. Bolt could see a speck off in the distance, but the light was not so bright, now that the surroundings were turning to their light gray tones. Bolt wanted to move faster, but Contra was taking his good old time, testing Bolt's cart. And Bolt dared not do anything that would upset him.

As they approached Solia's Palace, the desert faded behind them, and chalk-white patches dotted the ground. The floor transformed from a flat expanse into hills and valleys that grew larger and taller. The sky was the lightest gray Bolt had seen yet, except for the flame that Benecia had worn on her cloak. And the light above the palace became a beacon that began to fill Bolt's heart with hope.

Bolt told Scout to drop down for a closer look at the white patches. Contra's ghosts ignored them, so Bolt slipped off the cart to inspect the patches more carefully. The chalky spots now proved to be clumps of flowers on long slender stalks, waving in an apparent breeze that Bolt could not feel. The petals formed a tulip-like cluster with deep separations between the petals and an overall effect of a ring of fire.

When Bolt bent to touch the petals, they began to glow with a warm chalky light. When he touched them, the petals caressed his hand, and he felt a soothing reassurance sweep through his body. Yes, they were moving toward a better place.

As they drew closer, Bolt could first make out only the walls to the palace. Then the gate shone bright in the beacon's light that suspended itself above the gate. As they drew closer still, the high walls seemed to glow and grow, extending higher and higher above the palace they surrounded. Impressive. But the gate was closed. Would they be able to get in?

Contra landed in front of the gate. "Okay, I have delivered you. Don't forget to tell my sister that I rescued you."

Mad River Magic climbed out of their carts. Contra lifted off in Bolt's cart.

"Hey," yelled Bolt, "bring back my cart."

"I will keep it as collateral," said Contra, with a laugh, "until you keep your promise to help me take down Extor."

Contra and his ghosts zipped off into the distance at twice the speed Bolt thought the carts could fly. He sighed. Would their troubles never end? Well, at least they had reached Solia.

The gang approached the gate. Bolt pulled out the piece of paper and the card the server had given him. A door stood closed beside the gate. No stratoids were in sight, so Bolt knocked on the door.

The door opened and a stratoid stepped out. He was slight of stature and light gray. He wore an almost-white uniform, on the sleeve of which was a light gray embroidered flame.

"Who are you?" asked the guard in a monotone voice. "And what is your business?"

"We are Mad River Magic," answered Bolt, handing the guard the paper and card he had received from the server. "And we have escaped from Extor's Reception Center."

"So why do you come here?" continued the unimpressed guard.

"We want to talk to Solia," said Bolt, "to ask for her help in reaching Omni and finding a way back to our world."

"That's what they all say," said the guard with a sneer. "Actually there have been very few who have made it here from Extor's prison." He paused and appeared to spit, cleaning his mouth after voicing Extor's name. "Actually, you are the first to have made it all the way here. What a pity. You must have had help."

"We did, sir," said Bolt. "Benecia gave us instructions."

The guard seemed to regain interest.

"And Contra rescued us from the Desert of Indecision," continued Bolt.

"I wouldn't mention his name around here if I were you." The guard looked around to see if anyone was close by.

"May we speak to Solia?" asked Bolt.

"I let no one in without Solia's permission," said the guard, standing at attention.

Rey stepped up beside Bolt. "Would you please show Solia the paper and card, and tell her that we are hostages from the human world and are begging for her assistance?"

"As you wish," answered the guard, spinning and marching back through his door.

The gang looked at each other with worried faces. What else could they do now but wait? Bolt looked up at the towering wall. Surely the carts could fly over the top, but it was better to wait. The gate was massive. No chance of moving that. Could he open the guard door? Nope, the handle was inside.

They paced and waited and paced some more. What was taking so long?

Finally, the guard poked his head out of the door. "Permission denied. Go away."

"But how can we—"

Bolt's question was interrupted by the slamming of the door in his face. His heart sank. Why were every two steps forward accompanied by one step backwards?

He turned to face the gang. Scout's head was down, his foot scratching the ground. Lil's cheeks showed a stream of tears. Rey squinted with angry determination. And Bug was already trying to pull open the guard door.

"Come on," said Bolt. "We've made it this far. We won't give up. Let's fly around this palace until we find a more friendly guard. Benecia told us we would succeed. We just haven't found the right gate."

"Let's just fly over the top of the wall," said Bug, hopping into her cart. "Let's see if that wimpy guard can stop me."

"No," called Rey, "let's not ruin our reception. I vote to look all the way around the wall."

Everyone but Bug agreed, and Mad River Magic set out to explore the wall.

The palace was massive and as large as a small city. Surely there were other gates to this palace. Wow, those walls reached high into the sky. Why would Solia need such massive protection?

After flying for an hour, they had found no other gates or doorways. This place was strange. Halfway around the palace, a small trail headed off into the distance and over a hill, but there was no gate in the wall at that point. When the gang finally returned to their starting point, having traveled all the way around the palace, they had found no other entrance, no doors, and no windows.

Now what? Bolt hung his head trying to think of the way forward. It just did not make sense that Benecia would send them on a wild goose chase.

"Hey guys," yelled Bug. "Check this out."

She was high overhead, near the top of the wall. She swooped down to the gang and landed her cart.

"You won't believe what's on the other side of the wall," she said. She lifted off again, with the rest of Mad River Magic right behind her.

Bolt and Scout shot ahead to catch up with her. The gleaming walls stretched up three hundred feet. This was unbelievable.

When they reached the top, they stopped. Bug leaned back and smiled. Bolt's mouth dropped open. The rest of the gang sat in their carts in amazement. Inside the walls was...nothing. In the very center of the huge expanse sat a cluster of holographic lights, pointing at and painting the walls. Bolt leaned out of Scout's cart and touched the wall. Nothing. But he and Bug had touched the guard door. That didn't make sense.

Who was behind this cruel ruse? His anger rose. He was going to have a talk with that guard. He dropped back down to the entrance gate and swung out of the cart. As he turned to the guard door, Bolt noticed a strange look come over Scout's face. And when Bolt turned toward the door, it wasn't there. He pushed his hand through the wall where the door had been. A tingling sensation met his fingers. Becoming more angry, he walked into the wall. Rapid fire vibrations pushed him back, but he forced his way through.

Nothing. No guard, no door, no city. Turning back toward the wall, Bolt faced a hole the shape of his body piercing the imaginary perimeter. He stepped back through.

"We've been scammed," said Bolt. "Contra played us for fools."

"But where is the real Palace of Light?" asked Rey. "I believe Benecia. It has to be around here somewhere."

"Hey, gang," called Scout, from high above them, "come back up here."

Once again they flew to the top of the wall. This time Bolt hopped onto the back of Lil's cart. At the top, Scout was pointing into the distance.

"See that little road we noticed on the other side of this impostor?" said Scout. "Now follow it over the hill. See that little house with a light on top?"

The gang looked at each other. "Yes! Let's go."

They didn't even bother to fly around the fake palace, they headed straight for the little light. As they went over the hologram projection units at the center of the fake city, Bolt pulled out his wand with the new crystal.

"*Nenekilo!*[22]" he shouted.

A bright white light zapped the unit, and it exploded into dust. The entire fake wall disappeared, and the road they had originally followed narrowed into the little road winding over the hill.

---

[22] Pulverize! (nay-nay-kee-lo)

Chapter Twenty

Solia's Palace of Light

Mad River Magic quickly covered the remaining distance to Solia's palace. The road below remained narrow, rough, and steep, and the white fire-cluster flowers became thicker and thicker. As they approached their destination, the light became brighter, and now shone true white. This had to be the real deal.

When the gang arrived at Solia's palace, it was smaller than Bolt expected, not huge or pretentious, but clean and neat. Everything was bright white. Better still, the gate stood wide open, like welcoming arms.

Mad River Magic set down their carts and walked to the gate. Two greeters in white uniforms and flame-shaped hats welcomed them and ushered them into the palace.

The first thing Bolt saw was his cart. And behind it stood the most beautiful lady he had ever seen. Short and slender, with a gleaming white smile, a golden light seemed to radiate from her face. Her skin was dark brown, her hair black. She wore a flowing robe and hood that displayed every color of the rainbow. In her hand sparkled the source of the light, a white scepter with a flame-shaped tip.

The light was too bright to look at, but the presence of color in the gray Strata world was a feast for his eyes.

The gang instinctively bowed.

"Oh, no, no, my friends," said Solia. "Save your bows for Omni. I am simply Solia, the princess of good influence. Welcome to our village. We have been expecting you."

The gang looked at each other. How did she know?

Bolt looked at his cart.

"Oh, yes," said Solia. "We thought you might need this." She tapped the cart with her scepter. "We saw one of Contra's ghosts playing with it while he spied on us. We captured him and recovered the cart. Of course we bleached the nasty ghost as white as possible before we sent him back to Contra."

Laughter filled the air behind Solia. Dozens of nearly-white stratoids, looking like the server from the reception center, stepped out from their hiding places.

Bolt looked around the palace. Solia had called it a village, and it was small. The wall was low enough to jump over, even if you were on crutches. Everything was white, except Solia. The buildings were simple boxes, like Benecia's. The roads were shiny white without the dust, and flame-shaped flowers decorated yards and flower boxes everywhere.

A warmth and peace that he had not experienced since the gang had entered the Strata filled his heart. He sighed with contentment. Mad River Magic looked relaxed for the first time since they had entered the aperture.

Solia gave each member of the gang a welcoming hug. Lil got the most choked up with tears filling her eyes, and she didn't want to let go.

"You must be tired and hungry," said Solia, putting her arm around Lil's shoulders. "Come, we have prepared a meal for you. And then you shall sleep. You have been on a long journey. I know that you are very tired."

She ushered them into a large bright banquet room. The table was covered with real food, including all their favorites. Bolt couldn't remember when it was they had last eaten. It must have been over a day ago. No wonder his stomach was growling.

The gang sat down, Solia at the head of the table with Bolt and Rey next to her. She offered a simple prayer of thanks for Mad River Magic's safe travel and for the food. Then she asked for safety for the remainder of their journey. Bolt made a mental note. That's the way he would say his prayers in the future.

While they ate, Solia asked the gang about their world. She seemed particularly interested in how Gram and Gramps were doing. And she asked each member of the gang about themselves.

When Bolt slowed down from shoveling food into his mouth as fast as his stomach would accept it, he was ready to ask Solia questions about the Strata. He had so many. Where should he start?

"We were told by Benecia," said Bolt, "that Omni is the only one who can give us the key to reentering our world."

At the moment Bolt mentioned Omni's name, Solia and the stratoids briefly bowed their heads.

"That is correct," answered Solia. "And that is why it is so important that we spend the entire day tomorrow, when you are rested, preparing you for a successful remainder of your journey. There are still many dangers and challenges that lie ahead."

Bolt nodded in agreement. "What can you tell us about the Strata world? How did it come to be? Who is in charge? What is your position?"

"Young man," said Solia, with a beaming smile and patting Bolt's shoulder, "you are very inquisitive and, I can tell, very intelligent. Where your legs lack strength," she motioned to his crutches, "your mind more than makes up for it. We will talk about me and Contra and Extor tomorrow. As for Omni," she bowed her head, "you will have the opportunity to ask him those questions when you meet him. I will tell you that he created the Strata to be a good influence for people on the surface world, and he is the ultimate ruler. He is my father."

"Why does he allow Extor—"

"My son," Solia lifted Bolt's chin and peered deep into his eyes with a warm smile, "that is a matter that you should take up with my father. Extor is a thorn in the side of all of us. I fear that he is a putrid manifestation of that thing you call free will."

Bolt wasn't sure what she meant, but he got the message that it was time to quit asking questions. And, he decided, if he was stuck in this world, this would be a pretty neat place to live. Lil certainly was happy here. In fact, he got up and traded places with Lil so that she could sit closer to Solia. As he glanced back up the table at a very excited Lil, he noticed tears welling up in Solia's eyes. She tipped her head at him. Wow, this leader thing wasn't all bad stuff. That felt pretty good.

They finished their feast, and one of the stratoids showed them to the guest rooms, one for the boys and one for the girls. After showering to wash off the travel dust, Bolt and Scout crashed into bed. Before drifting off to sleep, Bolt glanced out the windows to see how Solia's palace operated during the darker hours. The streets were bare, and lights filled the windows of the houses. No one was going to or from work, except the guards in the watch towers that stood over the wall.

Bolt fell into a deep sleep with not a worry on his mind. He dreamed that an air raid siren was blaring and someone was knocking on his door. The knocking got louder.

Scout shook his shoulder. "Wake up!"

Bolt sat up, getting oriented. What was happening? He answered the door.

"Mr. Bolt," said the stratoid, "we need your help. Please dress and follow me quickly."

Bolt threw on his clothes and shoes, grabbed his crutches, and followed the stratoid. "What is going on?"

"Contra's ghosts are attacking," said the stratoid. "And they are trying to steal your carts. We need your help to move the carts to safety."

Bolt stick-hopped behind the stratoid to the wall of the village. The air raid siren continued to pierce the air. Blasts of lightning-like spears jumped from the canons mounted on the wall. The spears were accompanied by thunder as each spear shot off into the darkness. In the light produced by the spears Bolt saw the gray ghosts attempting to reach the carts. As each ghost approached, the thunder and lightning drove it away.

At the wall, the commander of the guard approached Bolt. "Sir, we need to move the carts into the village for their safety. My men do not know how to operate your carts. Would you move them for us? We will give you cover."

"I'll help, too," said Scout.

Bolt turned to find Scout behind him.

"Okay," said Bolt. "Just tell us when."

The commander gave the signal. A thunderous barrage of lightning spears exploded over the carts.

"Now!" yelled the commander.

Bolt and Scout raced to the carts. The turbo-levitators started. He whipped out his wand. "*Neekata!*" he yelled. The carts rose off the ground with Bolt and Scout in the lead, the other two carts following.

He was ready to move forward when he felt a tight grip on his wrist. Turning, he saw a ghost that had escaped the lightning spears. He couldn't reach for his wand with his hand restrained.

"Scout!" yelled Bolt.

Scout whipped out his wand and zapped the ghost with white light. The ghost relaxed his grip, and the carts shot forward.

Inside the village wall, the four carts were placed in a storage shed that was protected by the perimeter guards. Bolt hopped out and moved his cart into the shed, as well.

"Good work, my friends," said the commander. "If you ever want a job here in the Strata, just let me know."

Scout and Bolt shook hands with the commander. The air siren was turned off. And peace returned to The Palace of Light. Bolt and Scout returned to their room, dropped their clothes in a pile on the floor, and fell back into their beds.

The next morning, when the boys found their clothes cleaned and stacked neatly beside their bed, Bolt couldn't remember whether the dark hours adventure had been a dream or reality.

"Hey, Bolt," said Scout, "did we move our carts last night? I had the strangest dream."

The gang headed out for the banquet room and breakfast. As the dark hours dissipated and brightness returned to Solia's Palace, Bolt noticed a hill behind the village. On the hill sat a huge white bird guarding the runway. Wow, if he would have ignored the false signs and gone to Strata 333, they could have avoided a lot of grief. He would follow instructions more carefully from here on out.

Solia met them at the banquet hall and gave each member a hug. Lil was as excited as ever and insisted on sitting beside Solia.

Bolt wanted to ask questions, but Solia insisted they enjoy their breakfast. After breakfast they would move to a meeting room, and there would be time for a long discussion.

As they walked out of the banquet room, Solia suddenly stopped. "Oh, my." Her face became even brighter, the colors of her robe flashing like a neon sign. She shook her scepter at the sky. "He knows no boundaries. Omni must rein him in!"

Bolt looked up and saw the source of her anger. High in the sky, Extor's flying wolves trailed dirty gray smoke to write a message. "Do not attempt to go to Omni's Mountain. You will not survive. Return to my Reception Center, or you will die."

Solia pounded her scepter on the ground. "We shall show him, that dirty monster. Why, Omni, why?"

Solia led the gang into the meeting room, then called for her chief seamstress. Soon five stratoids, matching each of the gang in stature, stood beside Mad River Magic. The seamstress examined the stratoid uniforms the gang members were wearing, then took careful measurements of Solia's stratoids. And then the seamstress and her assistants were off to the sewing room.

"What are you doing?" asked Bolt.

"Two can play this game," she said. "Extor thinks he can easily defeat us because we are honest. Well, we are not lying, we are just creating decoys."

"What do you mean?" said Bolt.

"You shall see," said Solia. "We will take Extor on a wild goose chase while your gang escapes unnoticed to Omni's Mountain. Now come, we need to quickly go over some important instructions for your journey. We must hurry."

Solia and the gang sat at a round table. She gave each member a new wand tip, more powerful than the one they had received from Benecia. This tip would immobilize the enemy more quickly and for a longer period of time. Next, she placed a strange little box in front of each one of them. It had no discernible color, no buttons or switches. Only an aura of ever-changing color radiated from the box. Scout turned the box over and over, looking for clues.

"This is your Omni Box," said Solia. "Keep it in your pocket at all times. Do not allow it out of your reach. If you get into trouble, simply call for help, and Omni will respond."

She repeated the dangers of the Hemlock Forest, its water, and a particular creature that lived in the forest, the ringrac. She warned them that their carts would not fly over the forest, and that they must stay on the road. Above all else, they were instructed to stop for nothing, but continue until they reached Omni's Mountain.

Finally, she gave Rey letters of introduction to present to Omni.

When she finished, Bolt had to ask the obvious. "Why can't we just fly the white bird to Omni's Mountain?"

"I wish we could," said Solia. "But Omni does not have a lightport. Almost all of his visitors are spirit visitors, and they do not need an external form of transportation. But we will use the white bird to lead Extor's wolves away from your route of travel."

"Doesn't Extor know that there is no lightport at Omni's Mountain?" asked Rey.

"Extor and his followers are allowed nowhere close to Omni," said Solia. "He would have no way of knowing about the absence of a lightport."

Bolt's heart sank. He could see more challenges ahead. Man, couldn't anything be easy?

Solia finished her instructions, and the seamstress returned to the conference room followed by the five stratoids. Each of the five was dressed and disguised as one of the gang. Bolt looked at his counterpart. Wow, a wig and a bolt of white hair. Even matching crutches. The girls were examining their look-a-likes and inspecting the outfits. Scout was coaching his counterpart in making gestures.

"Come, we must hurry," said Solia. She led the gang to a second story window where they could watch the production.

Then she led the gang's impostors and their fake carts to the white bird. With much fanfare and lots of hugs, Solia sent off the fake gang on their journey back to the Reception Center. The gang held their breath, watching to see if Extor's wolves would follow.

Solia returned to Mad River Magic, and they watched together. But the wolves remained in the sky, circling Solia's Palace.

A new message, written in dirty dark gray, appeared just outside Solia's Palace.

"Nice try. Turn yourselves in. Or you will die."

Chapter Twenty-One

Flight Through the Omniflex Tunnel

"Time for Plan B," said Solia. "I knew Plan A might not work, but we had to try."

"So, what now?" asked Bug.

"Follow me," said Solia.

She led them to the entrance of the Conference building. There, a floating box truck unloaded its supplies and then took on new cargo in the form of Solia and the gang.

Rey pulled out her wand to call for the carts. Solia gently restrained her.

Putting her wrist to her mouth, Solia spoke into an invisible device. "Carts. Use the perimeter guards' convoy truck, lights flashing, and drive all the way out to the guard command post. Then meet us at the mine entrance."

The box truck glided smoothly over the white roads for ten minutes, then stopped. Sitting in the back of the truck, Bolt couldn't see where they were going. After the truck stopped and backed up, the door opened, and Solia hurried them into an old dilapidated, abandoned shack.

The gang looked around, confused.

"There is one route to Omni's Mountain," said Solia, "that Extor knows nothing about. This village sits over the site that Omni used to mine for omniflex, the building block of the Strata. There is a tunnel running from here to Omni's Mountain. Not even my stratoids know of it."

The convoy truck with the carts arrived and unloaded the carts. Solia sent off everyone else, then led the gang to the elevator.

"Before you descend," she continued. "There are a few more instructions I need to give you, things we did not cover before."

Mad River Magic gathered around her. Solia seemed to be worried for the first time. Bolt could tell that tension was building. This was to be the final leg of their journey, and it was obvious that Extor would do anything in his power to stop them.

As the gang leaned against their carts in front of the aged and unused elevator doors, Solia handed out a new device to each member.

"This is a light source for your travel through the tunnel," said Solia. "Put it on the front of your carts. There is no light in the tunnel. If you find a blockage in the tunnel, try the wand tips that I gave you previously. That should melt the omniflex. And most important, keep the Omni Box in your pocket at all times. If you need help, call Omni."

Bolt's mouth became dry. His palms started sweating. Mad River Magic looked at each other with tight lips. They had come this far. They weren't going to give up now.

Solia opened the ancient elevator door and helped move the carts in. She gave each member of the gang a hug. "I will keep Extor distracted as long as we can. I don't think there is anything he can do. But never underestimate the power of evil. I will also send a message to Omni and let him know you are on your way. When you get to the bottom of the elevator, take the tunnel that is straight ahead. Do not take any side trips. Do not stop for anything until you reach the bottom of his elevator at the other end. And when you get there, call on your Omni Box. He will send down his elevator for you."

The gang thanked Solia. The door closed, and the elevator lurched downward.

Everything quickly became dark. They turned on their light sources. The elevator bumped and banged. After what seemed like an eternity, the elevator seemed to bind and lurched to a stop.

Scout shone his light through the cracks in the door. "We're not down yet. There's no opening in front of us."

Rey looked at the control panel, but there were no buttons or lights, other than an up and down lever.

Bug finally grabbed the lever and pulled it up then quickly down. The elevator jerked and began its descent once again. The gang cheered.

Finally the elevator slowed and stopped. Bolt pushed the door open, and a large black opening with no light presented itself.

"Okay, gang," said Bolt, "let's see if our carts will fly down here."

The carts were lined up in single file, Bolt in the lead. Mad River Magic climbed in and turned on their turbos...nothing. Scout began making adjustments on his turbo, but nothing made the turbos work.

Rey pulled out her wand. "*Pemhanwi!*[23]" Nothing.

---

[23] It floats! (paym-hah-nwee)

Bolt pulled out his Omni Box and was contemplating using it, when he remembered the power of the elderly lady in the detention center. "By the power of Omni, let these carts fly to Omni's Mountain!" he shouted.

The rest of the gang looked at him as if he were mad. But a strange buzzing emanated from each cart, and they levitated a few inches off the tunnel floor. The gang cheered and climbed in. Bolt whispered a silent "Thank you," and they started down the tunnel.

An eerie cold echo tube surrounded them. At first Bolt moved cautiously through the tunnel. His light reached about one hundred feet into the darkness, and he didn't feel safe moving too quickly. But as he gained confidence, he picked up speed. And as his speed increased, so did the power of his headlight, piercing the blackness farther ahead. Soon the gang was zipping along at full speed, eager to reach Omni's Mountain.

Suddenly, a dark shadow jutted out from the side and into the path of the carts. Bolt slammed his turbo into reverse to decelerate and yelled at the gang. "Stop!"

The gang skidded to a silent stop in front of a massive projection of dark gray material oozing from the side of the tunnel. Scout was the first out of his cart to explore. He approached the shiny gray translucent lava flow cautiously. Stretching out his hand to feel for heat, then pulling out his wand, he touched the obstruction.

"Unknown compound." He announced. "It looks like the plastic that all of the Strata is built from. Let's try our wand tips that Solia gave us."

The gang piled out and readied their wands. Scout had already melted a hole in the dark gray mass.

"It melts easily," said Scout, "like drilling plastic."

Bolt and Rey surveyed the projection. It encroached on half of the space they needed to get by.

"Let's slice off back to this point," said Bolt. "If it's too heavy to move, we can chop it up into smaller pieces."

Bug jumped to the head of the line to go first. She sliced a groove halfway through the gray stuff. Scout went next and completed the cut. The material dropped to the floor of the tunnel with a loud thud. Bolt could tell that it was heavy from the sound, but the gang pushed together, trying to slide the obstruction out of the way. It didn't budge.

They sliced the massive piece in half. Still they couldn't move it. Finally, after quartering it, the gang was able to move the pieces out of the way.

Cheering with optimism, they hopped into their carts. They could do this. Hopefully they would reach Omni's Mountain soon. Wow, this had been a long battle.

After zipping along the tunnel another thirty minutes, Bolt saw a faint dot of light ahead. Could that be the bottom of the tunnel? Had Omni turned on the lights for them? Bolt turned up his turbo to top speed. Yes, they were almost there!

But something was wrong. The light was coming from the left side of the tunnel, not the top. And as they approached closer, the light opening looked jagged, rather than square or round. Bolt slowed his cart. Something didn't feel right. Couldn't anything go smoothly for once?

When they were almost at the opening, a strange shape moved into the light. Bolt stopped. They couldn't go back. He sighed. This leadership stuff was not his thing.

Turning to the rest of the gang, he pulled out his wand with Solia's tip. "Get ready for anything. I think we've got trouble."

Chapter Twenty-Two

Ringrac Invasion

*B*olt held his wand at ready, waiting for winged wolves to appear. Unusual chirps and bird calls echoed off the tunnel walls, becoming a background to louder barking and howling. Then, an even louder chattering and squeaking moved closer. It reminded Bolt of a combination of the raccoons he had heard in the forest, back at Cedar Heights, and the monkey chatter at the zoo. The clamor was quickly becoming deafening and seemed to surround them. Still he couldn't see anything.

The rest of the gang began shining their white lights onto the perimeter of the tunnel. Dark shadows flitted in and out of the light. The noise was closing in on them.

Suddenly, a shadowy figure swung out of the darkness above Bolt and dropped onto his cart. Before he could shine his white light on the attacker, both of his arms were immobilized by small, vice-like fists. A long tail wrapped around his neck and covered his mouth like a gag. He couldn't yell. The creature's light gray eyes shone in the night, but everything else was dark gray and difficult to see.

Bolt managed to turn his neck. Shiny eyes sat on each of the carts. The furry attackers' gray bodies revealed black spots. Their tails were long and ringed. Twisting back to look at the creature immobilizing him, he saw long dirty gray teeth, and a face that resembled a monkey with a nose that looked like a raccoon.

Before Bolt could survey the situation, the shiny eyes poured into the tunnel opening and surrounded them. Bolt's heart pounded loudly in his chest. What were they going to do this time? The muffled screams of Bug and Lil told him how helpless they all really were.

Suddenly the deafening chatter of the attackers became quiet. The mob of shiny eyes parted in front of him, and a larger creature approached Bolt. Its appearance resembled the others, but its gait instantly grabbed Bolt's attention. Swinging on long front arms, like a monkey, it reminded Bolt of walking with his crutches. The leader stopped in front of Bolt.

"I am Simi, king of the Ringracs," said the creature. "What are you doing in my cave?"

The ringrac holding Bolt loosened his tail so Bolt could speak.

"We are traveling to...," Bolt stopped. His mind was racing. This creature didn't know the tunnel extended to Omni's Mountain. What should he say?

"How did you get in here in the first place? Did you not read the sign that this cave was private property?" asked Simi.

"We are sorry for trespassing," answered Bolt. "We did not know this cavern belonged to you." He looked around. Escape didn't seem possible. "Would you please show us what route we can take to safely bypass your territory and get to the Palace of Light?" He dared not tell them that they were traveling to Omni's Mountain. Or should he?

Simi laughed then snarled at his soldiers, his chirping chatter was completely incomprehensible. His soldiers jerked Bug from her cart and led her, yelling and resisting, all the way to Simi.

"This spirited member of your group will make a worthy hostage," said Simi. "Now return from wherever you started, and this hostage will be unharmed. If you do not do as I say...well I won't tell you what we will do with her."

The whole group of ringracs burst out in laughter-like chatter.

Bolt looked around at the gang. What were they going to do? They couldn't leave Bug, but what would the ringracs do if the gang refused to leave? Bolt put his head in his hand, then realized the ringrac holding him had released his hands. Actually his captor had disappeared.

Looking again at the gang, Bolt now saw that all of the ringracs had disappeared, and the tunnel was empty. Rey and Lil were sobbing. Scout had slid down inside his cart.

Bolt moved out through the opening into a dark woods. The Hemlock Forest. Ahead, Bolt could hear the trees bending and swishing, as the ringracs swung through the forest. Their chatter and squeaking quickly became fainter.

A cold sweat broke out on Bolt's face. They didn't have a choice. They had to rescue Bug. But what if...? He didn't want to think of it.

"Come on, gang," called Bolt. "Let's get moving."

"But what will they do to Bug if they find we are following?" asked Rey, wringing her hands.

"I want to go home," murmured Lil, her head down, tears streaming down her cheeks.

Scout said nothing. But his cheek was wet where he had wiped a tear.

"I know we have no good choice," said Bolt. "But we're a team. We stick together. If you were Bug, would you want us to try to rescue you?"

Bolt climbed back into his cart and turned into the forest. His cart rose above the Hemlock trees. That was a good sign. Solia didn't have all the answers. But that was scary, too. What else was she wrong about? They needed to catch up with the ringracs before it became completely dark. He turned to check that all the gang was following him. Rey was bringing up the rear with her wand pointed behind her. Bug's empty cart followed.

Now was the time when they could use Bug's courage to take on the enemy. He needed to come up with a plan, and he needed to do it quickly.

Ahead he could see a ripple in the Hemlocks, like a breeze or wave moving through the forest. That must the ringracs. He slowed and gathered the gang. He didn't have a good plan, but it was the only thing he could think of. At least they now had the carts flying, so they had the element of surprise. They could do this.

Bolt and Scout came in first, buzzing the ringracs and spraying them with their paralysis lights. Rey and Lil would then release Bug.

It didn't work. Instead of being immobilized by the light, the ringracs dropped from their trees onto the carts. Bolt shoved and kicked and managed to knock several ringracs from his cart before he shot above the trees. Scout struggled behind him, but did manage to break free and follow him.

They swung in a circle and came in for another pass. But what they saw stopped them cold. In a clearing, with their wands held by ringracs and illuminating the scene, Bug and Rey and Lil hung from trees like Christmas ornaments, upside down with their arms and legs stretched out on a miniature circular rack. Simi stood beside Bug, a long knife in his hands, the tip against Bug's chest.

Bolt slammed on his brakes and skidded to a stop.

"I thought you would see the error of your ways," said Simi, with an evil smile on his face. "Now tie up those two as well," he commanded his soldiers.

Scout and Bolt were ripped from their carts and quickly bound and hung up beside the girls. Simi removed the gags from the girls' mouths so that Bolt could hear them crying.

"Not a pretty sound," he said, laughing as he approached Bolt. "Since you didn't obey my order, I think you will be first on the menu tonight."

The ringracs jumped up and down on tree branches and chattered loudly.

Everything was going red. Bolt could hardly think. It was over. Why didn't Extor just kill them back at the visitor's center? Why all this torture? Hopefully there would be little pain...No! They couldn't give up. Solia had said they could succeed. They still had some other route for escape. But what was it?

Bolt strained and twisted. Scout's Omni Box was visible in his pocket, and Bolt managed to grab it with his mouth. Simi stood back and howled with laughter. Bolt mumbled a garbled message into the Omni Box, "Help! We're caught by the ringracs in the Hemlock Forest." He dropped back to hanging vertically, released the box, and breathed a prayer for a quick death.

Simi picked up the box and slapped Bolt across the face. "Enough of your antics, you fool," he yelled. "It is time for you to die. My men are hungry." The trees exploded with excited chatter. He grabbed his knife and raised it over his head.

A pure white bolt of lightning flashed across the sky, followed immediately by thunder so loud it shook the trees. The ringracs dropped from their perches and huddled together, looking fearfully at the sky. Another volley of lightning bolts struck the clearing with deafening thunder so powerful that it threw Simi backwards. Shaking, Simi stepped back into the opening and looked up. A whistling sound like a coming storm filled the air. A breeze quickly gave way to a strong wind, and the trees bent back and forth. The ringracs scurried away on the ground.

Simi turned to Bolt, pointing his knife at him. "We shall meet again. And the next time you will be mine." He turned and sprinted with a swinging gait after his soldiers.

Fluttering of wings filled the air over the clearing, and a crowd of angels settled gently into the clearing. Bolt blinked repeatedly. Yes, this was really happening. The girls stopped crying.

The angel commander stepped forward. His white shimmering body and wings were translucent like the other stratoids, but they glittered as if giving off light. His lower body was wrapped in a robe. His upper body was bare with strong thick wings folded on his back.

"I am Tutoro, the captain of Omni's seventh company of angels. Omni sent us to rescue you from the ringracs."

The angels quickly released the gang from the racks and placed them on the ground. Bolt waited a moment for the dizziness to pass and his head to clear.

"Thank you," said Bolt. "I didn't know if Omni would hear me."

"Omni always hears when his subjects call for help," answered Tutoro. "Now tell me how you came to be captured by the ringracs."

Bolt told him the whole story from being caught in the aperture, to capture by Extor, to escape and travel to Solia's palace, ending with the capture in the tunnel.

Tutoro rubbed his chin, deep in thought. "That is quite a story. I don't believe I have ever heard of a situation similar to yours. There have been many of Extor's prisoners who have refused to obey him, and their spirits have been transported to

Omni's mountain, where they are given refuge. But there have never been any prisoners who have escaped and arrived in both body and spirit."

Bolt's heart sank. If this was new, would Omni be able to return them to their world?

"Can you take us to Omni's Mountain?" asked Rey, stepping forward and presenting letters that Solia had given her. "We would be very grateful if you would help us."

Tutoro read over the letters and smiled at Rey. "We would be honored to escort you to the mountain. I think you will find it to be the most beautiful place you have ever seen. And Omni will be able to help you, if anybody can."

Tutoro and his angels inspected the carts with interest.

"So these devices can fly?" asked Tutoro.

"Yes, sir," answered Scout. "Would you like me to show you what they can do?"

"You can show us on the way to Omni's Mountain," said Tutoro. "Let's get out of this dark forest and back to the light."

Chapter Twenty-Three

Angel Escort

Mad River Magic mounted their carts and lifted off with the angel escort. Tutoro led the way. Each cart was flanked by twenty angels. They flew over, under, and around the carts, asking questions of the gang, and they laughed loudly when Bug did some vertical loops and barrel rolls. Tutoro finally had to remind his men of the need for decorum. The angel flying beside Lil smiled and winked at her, then kept a straight face.

As the carts flew higher above the Hemlock Forest, Bolt noticed a glowing white cloud in the distance. As the group got closer to the cloud, it became brighter and brighter. Finally a shining white city could be seen towering on top of a high mountain. Hope once again filled Bolt's chest. They were almost there. Omni had to have the answers they needed.

But when the group arrived at the base of the mountain, Bolt saw that their struggles weren't over yet. The mountain gleamed of white quartz, unlike the omniflex everything else was made of, and it was slippery and steep. Looking up the mountain, Bolt lost confidence that their carts could fly that high. And the gang certainly couldn't climb the steep vertical walls of the mountain.

"What now?" asked Bolt, looking at Tutoro. "How could anyone climb this mountain?"

Tutoro smiled at Bolt. "You are correct. No one can scale this wall without our assistance, not even Solia. But we are here to help you."

Four angels surrounded each cart, lifting it and its occupant straight up. Mad River Magic soared above the clouds as Omni's city became brighter and brighter. When they reached the top, Tutoro and his company set the gang down at the gate to the city and disappeared.

Mad River Magic shielded their eyes from the blinding light as they checked out their new surroundings. The walls sparkled with colorful gems. The path to the main gate was white. And the gate shimmered like pearls.

Bolt and Rey approached the gate with Solia's letters. Bolt swallowed hard and knocked on the gate. An angel materialized in front of them.

"Welcome to Omni's Mountain," said the angel. "What do you want?"

"We have come to see Omni," answered Bolt.

Rey handed the angel their letter of introduction.

After glancing over the letter, the angel handed it back to Rey, unimpressed. "Do you have an appointment with Omni?"

Bolt and Rey looked at each other, confused.

"I thought Solia had made arrangements for us," said Rey.

The angel yawned and scratched his head. "I think Solia is sending a group that will be arriving via the elevator. Omni is expecting them, but I have been told of no group that is arriving at our gate. I'm sorry."

And the angel quickly disappeared back through the gate.

Bolt and Rey looked at each other again. Tears formed in Lil's eyes. Scout hopped out of his cart and approached the gate. He reached forward cautiously and touched the pearly surface. It resisted his hand.

Bug jumped out of her cart and strode to the gate. She pulled her Omni Box out of her pocket. "Omni, your honor, sir, thank you for rescuing us from the ringracs. We were supposed to arrive via the elevator, but Tutoro has delivered us to your main gate. Please, may we come in, sir?"

Scout hung his head. Rey put her arm around Lil's shoulders to comfort her. Bolt pulled his Omni Box from his pocket.

"Please, sir," he whispered.

Instantly a deep booming voice filled the mountain, "Let them come in!"

The gate divided in the middle and swung open from both sides. Mad River Magic pulled their carts into Omni's Mountain and stopped, staring in amazement.

The street stretched as far as they could see into the horizon. Although constructed of the same omniflex material, it emanated a golden light. White buildings lined the street with golden light piercing their windows. The gang shielded their eyes. It was too bright to take it in.

A smiling angel approached the gang and gave each of them a pair of glasses. "These are your Omni glasses. They will protect your eyes from the bright light until you become accustomed to it."

With the glasses on, objects that had appeared blinding white were now a rainbow of colors. The street was still translucent, transmitting a golden glow. And the sky was the whitest white Bolt had ever seen. Objects that were a blur, now came into focus.

In front of the buildings, bright green foliage covered the ground, with white, flame-shaped tulip-like blooms scattered everywhere. The buildings were now a spectrum of every color imaginable, gleaming in the white light that bathed everything.

Angels flew back and forth, seemingly busy with tasks they were intent on. Like Tutoro, they were translucent and glimmered with their own light. And like Tutoro, they were white. But with his glasses on, Bolt noticed the angels glowed with an iridescence of a full spectrum of colors.

Wow, this place was intense. Bolt turned around, trying to take it all in. No shadows. Somehow he knew there could be no period of darkness in this city, no night.

Bolt and Mad River Magic stood in awe, overcome and paralyzed with the beauty.

When they began walking down the street, they started seeing humanoids, or at least they looked like humans. Only now their bodies were translucent, like the stratoids. They wore white robes. And they were singing music like Bolt had never heard before, beautiful harmony that made him want to sing with them. No, he kept his mouth shut. He couldn't sing.

Someone behind him began singing. Lil. She was belting out the melody perfectly. He had never heard her sing before.

"Where did you learn to sing like that?" he asked her.

"I don't know," said Lil. "It just came out. It feels so good."

Rey and Bug joined in. Perfect harmony. Bolt raised his eye brows and turned to Scout. He shook his head with a grin. Bolt agreed.

And then a voice boomed from the sky. Actually it seemed to fill the entire space around them. "Welcome to Omni's Mountain, Mad River Magic. We have been expecting you. I apologize for my sleepy guard at the front gate. He must have slept through the daily briefing.

"Please continue down the golden street. We have a house prepared for you," continued Omni. "You will know it when you see it. I trust that your stay with us will be nourishing, and will fortify you for the battle you have chosen. We will meet after you have settled in, eaten, and rested."

Bolt spun slowly while Omni was speaking, but could see no evidence of where Omni was. The rest of the gang had a peaceful look on their faces. The worry lines were gone. Even Rey appeared to have let down her guard. She and Lil were hugging. Bug resumed singing loudly, apparently impressed with her new-found vocal talent. It was beautiful, but Bolt wished she had a volume control that he could turn down.

Scout was absolutely ecstatic with all the new things to explore, looking for the source of power to the golden-light street, dissecting the flame-shaped tulips, rubbing his fingers everywhere looking for dust, holding his hand up and looking for a shadow. Man, he wasn't going to want to leave this place.

Bolt smiled. What a place. Was this heaven?

Then he saw her, a little white-haired lady wearing a shimmering white robe, her skin a radiant light brown. She approached them with wide open arms and a huge smile. She pulled the gang together and gave them a tight hug. The little lady on the rack!

"Welcome to Omni's Mountain," said the feisty little lady. "I see you have found the path to the light." Turning to Bolt, she continued. "I sensed that night on the rack that you wanted to stand to protect me. I saw Mr. Finkelstein push down on your shoulder. Thank you, my son. But now you see that I have found a much better place."

Not knowing what to say, Bolt hugged the little lady and said simply, "Thank you. But how do you know me?"

With a twinkle in her eye, she said, "Omni shares his knowledge." Then turning to the rest of the gang, "I am Anna. I was in the containment center the night Bolt was there. You have a good leader. I understand that you are seeking to return to the earthly world. You will be a great force for good when you return. Just remember the power that fills you."

The gang looked nervously at each other, not sure what to say.

"Are you returning to the earthly world?" said Bolt.

"No," said Anna, "I will stay here until Omni decides that I am ready to move on."

"Where will that be?" said Rey. "This seems like such a lovely place."

Anna smiled and sighed. "I don't know. I am okay with whatever he wants me to do."

"Is...this...heaven?" said Scout in a quiet voice.

"I thought it was when I first arrived here," said Anna. "But, no, Omni's Mountain is not heaven. I hope that is where Omni will send me when I have finished my work here. I think he likes my approach to greeting the new arrivals."

"What new arrivals?" said Bolt. "I thought Tutoro and Solia said that they had seen no other escapees make it to Omni's Mountain."

"That is correct," said Anna. "But there are many who have refused to bend to Extor's demands. And Omni transports them here."

"I thought Extor threatened to remove their essence of free will," said Bolt.

"Extor can remove their essence of free will," said Anna, "and return a fake body to the earthly world. But he cannot remove the soul. His power only lies in darkness. When you return to the earthly world, and I have no doubt that you will succeed, I hope you will be an ambassador for light."

Bolt remained quiet. He wasn't sure what all this meant. But he liked the part where she was confident they would make it back to earth. Which made him suddenly think, where was this place?

But before he could continue with the questions, Anna put her arm around Lil's waist and led them down the golden street.

"I will show you your new quarters," she said. "I think you will be pleased. You might even decide you want to stay here."

Hmm. This place was amazing, but why would someone not want to return to their home and family? He had more questions for Anna if Omni wouldn't answer them.

Side by side with Lil, Anna led them until they stood in front of what had to be their house. Omni had said they would know, and Omni was right. How did he know?

In front of them stood a large gleaming white duplicate of Cedar Heights. Over the front door, instead of numbers for a street address, were the letters "MRM." And beside the house was a miniature car port with five stalls, sized perfectly for their barrel carts.

Rey pointed her wand, and the carts filed into their respective slots.

Anna watched in amazement, then stood in front of Rey. "May I see your wand?

Rey reluctantly handed her wand to Anna and watched carefully.

"Where did you get your wands?" asked Anna. "And who taught you to use them?" She looked at the rest of the gang to see if they each had a wand.

"Our Gram and Gramps from Cedar Heights gave them to us," said Rey, turning to look at the replica of Cedar Heights. "They also taught us how to use them. Plus Gramps had some ancient magic books in his library that we studied."

"Ah," said Anna. "That explains something. Let me show you the inside of your house."

She led the way through the front door of Cedar Heights, and Mad River Magic eagerly followed.

Inside, the gang came to an abrupt halt. Everything looked exactly the same as back home. Bug and Scout raced to the family room and the kitchen.

"Hey, guys. Come look at this," Bug yelled.

Rey and Bolt hurried into the family room. Lil took Anna's hand and pulled her along.

Wow, it was amazing. Bolt stared in disbelief. In front of them stood life-size statues, if that's what you could call them, of Gram and Gramps. Like the stratoids, they were translucent. Like the angels, they shimmered white. Bolt took off his glasses and approached the statues. They were perfectly still.

"Why are Gram and Gramps here?" asked Bolt. "Are they really here, or are they statues?"

"They are not here," answered Anna. "They are holographs, and Omni put them here to make you feel at home."

Bolt rotated, doing a three-hundred-and-sixty-degree survey. Man, it was amazing how everything was exactly the same as back home.

"How did Omni—"

"Omni knows everything," said Anna. "He is omniscient."

A statue, or rather a holograph, on the mantle caught Bolt's attention. He and Rey approached it together. A miniature white-robed wizard with long blond hair and blue eyes held an exact replica of their wand, pointing at them and gazing deep into their eyes. They looked at each other, shrugging and shaking their heads.

"Who is this?" asked Rey. "This wasn't on the mantle at Cedar Height."

"That's what I was talking about when I said 'that explains something,'" said Anna. "That is the Wizard of Cedar Crest. I wonder if he was the original owner of your grandfather's magic books. Omni said that the wizard was one of the great light magicians. We'll have to ask Omni for more of his history."

Bolt and Rey looked at each other, nodding with understanding. Why hadn't Gramps shown them a picture of the old wizard? Ah, maybe there weren't any pictures. Maybe Omni was the only one who knew what the wizard looked like. But why did Omni put the statue here? And what plans did Omni have for them? Bolt rubbed his chin, deep in thought.

"Bolt, Bolt," someone called him from his thoughts. "Look what Anna fixed for us." It was Bug, standing at the large round kitchen table, pointing at Bolt's favorite breakfast, buckwheat pancakes and maple syrup."

"How did you know?" Bolt asked Anna, with an expression of amazement.

"Omni shares his knowledge," answered Anna, grinning, with a twinkle in her eye. "Now sit down and eat. You have a day full of learning tomorrow and a long journey yet ahead of you."

The gang quickly took their usual seats and lifted their forks to dig in.

"Ah, ah, ah. Now what are we forgetting?" Anna stopped them in mid stab.

"The prayer," said Lil, smiling at Anna.

"Who would like to say the prayer this morning?" said Anna, looking around the group.

The gang hesitated. Bolt raised his hand. "I'll say it." He remembered Solia's prayer. "Dear Heavenly Father, thank you for bringing us safely to Omni's Mountain. Thank you for Anna and this food she has prepared. Please give us safety as we travel back to our Cedar Heights. Amen"

The gang and Anna echoed the amen. And then Mad River Magic created a flurry of forks and flying pancakes as the stack at the center of the table spread out onto individual plates and into hungry mouths.

Within fifteen minutes, Bolt was leaning back in his seat and rubbing his full stomach. Now that was a breakfast. He glanced at the kitchen. Would they have to wash the dishes? Anna seemed to know his every thought? She pulled Rey to her feet and handed her the wand Anna had admired.

"Would you do the honors, my dear?" Anna winked at Bolt as she addressed Rey.

Rey handed the wand back to Anna. "Point at the dishes."

Anna pointed.

"Now say '*Kithilo!*[24]'" said Rey.

"*Kithilo!*" commanded Anna.

The hot water turned on and filled the kitchen sink. The dish washing soap inverted and squirted soap into the water. The plates and forks lifted from the table and filed one-at-a-time to the kitchen and through the soapy water. They dipped themselves into the rinse water, danced with the dish towel, then stacked themselves on the shelf or into the silverware drawer.

The gang cheered, and Anna gave Rey a hug, handing her wand back to her.

"I simply must ask Omni for a wand," said Anna. "How could I ever get along without one?"

Mad River Magic clapped again. Anna took a bow.

"Now my young charges," said Anna, "it is time for some sleep. You want to be well-rested and at peak performance when you meet Omni tomorrow morning. You have much knowledge to cram into your heads before the final battle."

The gang, minus Bolt, headed for their rooms. Where was he to sleep? He had never stayed overnight at Cedar Heights, except when they camped out. He glanced at Anna.

"Come," she said. "I will show you."

She led him to the library, where his bedroom from home magically appeared.

"Sleep well," said Anna. "I will see you in the morning."

Bolt plunked down on the bed. He really was tired. So many battles to fight. Anna had said "the final battle."

He leaned back against his pillow and was closing his eyes, when he noticed the two pictures on his dresser. He sat up. Two? There was only one at home. He hopped out of bed.

The one on the left was his mother. He picked up the picture and gave his mother a kiss.

"We're trying to get back home, Mom." A tear formed in each eye. He wiped his eyes with his sleeve. "I love you, Mom."

Who was the other picture? Hopefully not Jerk. Bolt picked up the picture. A young man, tall and skinny with red hair and freckles, smiled back at him. Wow, it almost looked like him. Dad? He hadn't seen any of his dad's younger pictures since Jerk moved in. Bolt touched his father's face, and the picture changed. A slightly older version of his father met him, this one with crutches. This picture showed the stress in his father's face. Bolt began tapping the pictures and watched the progression of the disease. As his father's legs became weaker, the smile became

---

[24] Wash! (kee-thee-lo)

dimmer. Bolt's stomach tightened, thinking of his future. But curiosity made him continue.

The final picture was that of an elderly angel with white wings and white hair. One bolt of red hair stood rudely on top of his head. The strong smile had returned to his face. Bolt touched the picture gently, and the angel jumped from the frame. A holographic image fluttered to the top of the mirror, and an image wrote itself on the mirror.

"Sleep well, my son. We are watching over you."

Chapter Twenty-Four

Omni's Mountain

*B*olt woke to a bell ringing. It sounded just like the one Gram rang at Cedar Heights when it was time for a meal. He jumped out of bed and looked for a shower that wasn't occupied. The mud room was empty, and he took a quickie shower, as his mom called it, running hot water over his body, then toweling off. He didn't want to miss out on another breakfast.

Back in the library bedroom, he found a new uniform neatly folded and lying on his dresser. White undergarments and a white robe. It didn't shimmer like Anna's, but wow, it was bright.

He slipped on his new clothes, and turned to his dad's holograph. "What do you think, Dad?"

A new message appeared on the mirror. "I'm proud of you, son. Listen carefully to everything Omni tells you, and you will make it back to Cedar Heights."

Bolt had so many questions he wanted to ask his dad. Maybe there would be time tonight, or rather during the sleep hours. He rushed out to breakfast.

"Good morning, Bolt." Anna greeted him as he slid into his spot at the table. "For breakfast this morning, we have a taco omelet and refried beans."

Bolt stared at Anna in amazement. "How did you know?"

"According to Omni," said Anna, "this is your second favorite breakfast."

Rey turned to Bolt. "Why do you get to have your favorite breakfasts?"

Bolt blushed. Anna was treating him special. Why?

"What would you like for supper tonight?" asked Anna, as she stood behind Rey's chair. "Let's see, Omni said you like cheeseburgers and green peppers."

Now it was Rey's turn to blush. "That sounds great," she said. "Thanks."

While Mad River Magic chowed down on breakfast, Anna went over the schedule and instructions for the day.

She ended with the admonition, "It is vital that you follow all of Omni's instructions if you are to be successful in returning to your earthly world."

That reminded Bolt. "Where exactly is this Strata world?"

"Save your questions for Omni," answered Anna. "We need to get moving. You don't want to keep Omni waiting. Now realize that you may not be able to understand the reasoning behind all of Omni's instructions. Your earthly knowledge is very limited. You only need to follow his instructions."

Outside their house, Rey paused at the cart port. "Do we need to bring our carts?"

"Oh, yes," said Anna, "I think Omni has some special tools to improve your carts."

Rey pointed her wand behind her, and the carts followed in single file.

Bug jumped and twirled in her new robe, making it lift as it spun around her.

"We have now established that centrifugal force is operational here on Omni's Mountain," said Scout. "So, Bug, it is now time to be a little more lady like."

Bug stuck out her tongue and spun faster.

Lil turned and smiled at the gang as she took the lead with Anna, clinging to her hand.

Bolt brought up the rear with Rey. He shook his head. Was it really possible that this gang was going to be successful in returning to Cedar Heights?

As the gang hustled to keep up with Anna, they moved closer to the center of the city. The glowing golden road became wider. The buildings stood larger and taller. More angels and humanoids shared the street, their white wings or robes flowing as they glided down the avenue. The singing became louder and more beautiful. Even Scout seemed to be trying to sing. Bolt wasn't ready to try that yet.

As they reached the center of the gleaming iridescent city, a huge shining tower came into view. Anna delivered them to the front door. "The Omni Center" was announced in huge gold letters.

"I will see you this evening," said Anna. "Now listen very carefully, and do everything Omni tells you."

Mad River Magic stepped through the front door and looked around. Now what?

A buzzing, like static on a radio, filled Bolt's head. He could tell the others heard it as well, because they were rubbing their ears. Then the sound became crystal clear.

"Welcome to my mountain and the Omni Center," said a deep baritone voice. Bolt glanced at the gang. They were nodding their heads. They heard it, too.

"Proceed to the elevators in front of you," said the voice.

The gang walked across the large lobby, their carts floating behind them. They punched the button. The door slid open, presenting a huge elevator with enough room for them and their carts.

"Punch button number seven," said the voice.

Scout hit the button, the door closed, and the elevator began a slow ascent.

"While you are riding the elevator, let me introduce myself," said the voice. "I am Omni, and I will personally train you for the completion of your journey back to Cedar Heights."

The elevator stopped at the seventh floor. The bell rang, and the door opened.

"Turn right and proceed to conference room number three," said Omni.

"Wow, this is some hotel," thought Bolt.

"Thank you, Bolt," said Omni. "I wanted the best facility to train humanoids who arrive here.

"Did he just hear Bolt's thoughts?" The voice was Rey's, but her mouth wasn't moving.

"Yes, Rey," said Omni, "and I can hear your thoughts as well. In fact we are in conference mode. So I can hear the thoughts of all of you. This way of communicating cuts through the unnecessary words that clutter and hide the truth. Much more efficient."

"Okay, Bug," thought Scout, "be careful what you think. You are talking to God."

A deep baritone chuckle filled their ears. "Thank you, Scout," said Omni. "But I am not God."

Before he could stop his thoughts, Bolt asked, "Then who are you, Omni?"

"Yea, who are you?" thought Rey. Then she looked surprised and put her hand over her mouth.

"That is a fair question, Bolt and Rey," said Omni. "I am the ruler of the Strata world. But I am not God. He gave me power over the voices in your mind that influence your behavior, the exercise of your free will. Fortunately or unfortunately, depending on how you look at it, that free will has unleashed a powerful force in Extor, who is constantly trying to lead you down the wrong path. My daughter, Solia, is in charge of the good influences. And I try to keep them in balance, an ever more difficult undertaking. We'll talk more about that later today."

The gang had reached Conference Room 3.

"Please enter and have a seat," said Omni.

Mad River Magic entered. They all thought, "Wow!"

The group stood, transfixed in total amazement. Bright warm light filled the room, but did not hurt their eyes. They took off their glasses. The conference room was arranged like Extor's, in a semicircle, with rows of seats forming an arena. But the room was much smaller than Extor's.

"Why is this room smaller than Extor's," thought Bolt.

Again Omni chuckled. "A good question, Bolt. There are far more humans who choose to follow Extor's influence rather than follow Solia's."

"But where are they?" thought Bolt. "I mean the followers of Solia."

"They are here on my mountain," said Omni. "And we have training sessions for them in this room, too. But all of them have decided to stay or transition to Heaven. Today we are having a special session for you, because you wish to travel back to earth."

"Okay," thought Rey, "so how do we get back to earth?"

"Another good question, Rey," said Omni. "That will take all day to answer. You do realize, first of all, that you don't have to return. You have refused to bend to Extor, and you can remain here."

"Wow," thought Scout, looking around, "this would be a neat place to explore."

"Check out those seats, Scout," said Omni.

Scout sat in the seat in front of him. Immediately it began going up and down until it placed him at exactly the right height for his arms. The arm rests adjusted. A foot rest adjusted to support his feet. A computer pad appeared on the desk in front of him. Turning to the gang, Scout smiled and looked for more buttons to push. A cable coiled beside the computer, one end connected to an electrode. Beside the cable, a sign stated "memory download."

Scout spun his chair around, looking at Rey and Bolt. "Couldn't we stay here for awhile, just to get acquainted?"

"No!" said Lil. "I want to get home to Grams. I want to see Mom and Dad."

"Okay," said Omni. "Let's get started. Everyone find a seat."

As Mad River Magic chose seats, a curtain on the stage slid back, revealing a huge screen. Unusual background music filled their ears with Omni's voice easily heard over the music. His deep baritone voice kept their attention. A movie or video began to unfold on the screen, pulling them deeper into the Strata. Omni narrated as the story of the Strata began. Brief glimpses of the creation of the Strata gave the gang a good overview of the layout of this world, Omni's mountain on the light side, Extor's palace on the dark side. Solia's palace was closer to Omni's mountain on the light side. Contra's Cavern stood on the dark side, close to Extor. And all throughout the Strata, stages were crowded together, stacked in layer after layer, one strata on top of another.

"Is it okay to interrupt to ask a question?" thought Bolt.

The video paused. "Yes, Bolt, you may ask a question," said Omni.

"Sorry," thought Bolt. "Where did Extor come from? And why did he take power from Contra?"

"Good question." Said Omni. "Contra is my son, the dark sheep of the family. He chose to be the influence for evil, and he served in that position for millennia. But evil has grown steadily stronger and more appealing. Extor rose as a dark force from within Contra's ranks, willing to fill that void. Extor's hunger for control and recognition knows no limits. He is constantly bending or breaking the rules. The creation of channels connecting to earth, like the one that trapped you and brought you to the Strata, is an example. I am continually reining him in, and Contra is continually attacking him, trying to regain power."

"Why is everything gray?" asked Scout.

"That is a good question, Scout, and one that I am asked frequently," answered Omni. "First, you noticed that the white light, here on my mountain, contains all the colors of light when viewed through the prism glasses that you were given. So, here on Omni's Mountain, we have all the colors of the rainbow.

"And you noticed, when you met my daughter Solia, that her face was brown. When you mix all colors of pigment, the result is brown. So, in Solia's Palace of Light, all colors are present as well.

"Now, you noticed that Extor is nearly black, the absence of light. And the spectrum between white—all colors of light—and black—no light—is gray. That spectrum of gray represents the influence the Strata coaches are giving people back in your world, from light, good influence, to dark, bad influence.

"Does that make sense?" asked Omni.

"I think so," said Scout, scratching his head.

"Why can't we see Omni?" thought Lil, then startled that her thoughts were played in her ears.

"Lil," said Omni, "you have found the importance of connection, love, and touch. That is why humans have each other. I am actually in this room with you. But you cannot see me because my body is of a form that is invisible to your eyes. Sometimes, for very special people, I put on a human form."

A nebulous cloud swirled around Lil and gradually coalesced into an elderly man with flowing white hair and a long white beard. His robes gleamed with white light. He settled beside Lil, putting his arm around her shoulders and planting a kiss on top of her head. Lil's face reflected the warmth and light. Then Omni returned to his invisible state. The smile on Lil's face looked like it would never disappear.

Omni continued the video and overview of the Strata. By the end of the morning Bolt felt like he understood the forces that would face the gang when they left Omni's Mountain.

They broke for lunch, and Omni directed them to the cafeteria. As they walked out the doors of the conference room, Omni's voice had one final invitation. "Scout, you and the gang are welcome to explore the center. I will meet you back here after your lunch."

As they walked down the halls, Bolt felt a temptation creeping into his thoughts. This place was so beautiful. Why not just stay here? Scout was touching everything and absolutely delighted with so many things to explore. Rey's face no longer contained the stress that had filled it with wrinkles up until now. Bug was twirling and dancing, trying to fly like the angels who glided by them. And Lil, that broad smile on her face would never wash off. So why fight the battle? If Omni would let them stay here, why not stay? Man, this leadership thing was no fun. Hopefully, tonight he could ask his dad some questions.

The cafeteria drew them in with the smells of delicious food. The room wasn't big, and it was almost empty, but it was stocked with all their favorite foods. Apparently it was just for them. The angels apparently didn't need to eat. And the stratoids? Bolt had never seen them eating, either.

The rest of the gang chattered excitedly as they ate. Bolt was deep in thought. This was a difficult decision.

When Mad River Magic returned to the conference room for the afternoon session, Omni began laying out specifics of the journey they must take.

"Understand that you are embarking on a difficult trip," said Omni. "The journey back will not be the same route that you took before, and the channel back to earth will not be the same one that brought you here. You will not be able to take anything back with you that you did not bring here."

"What about Finkelstein?" Bolt thought.

"The one exception is Finkelstein, and something else I am going to give you later," continued Omni. "I will permit you to take Finkelstein back. But realize that this will make your trip much more challenging. And, if you don't take him back, he will end up here, so consider carefully whether you want to add that challenge."

"But we have to," thought Bolt.

"Your loyalty is commendable, Bolt," said Omni. "I will assist you."

A map appeared on the screen, revealing a narrow road meandering through the Hemlock Forest and past Contra's Cavern. It continued through the Desert of Indecision and skirted Extor's Palace of Darkness. At that point there was a small branch that divided from the road and led to Extor's Palace. And finally the small road ended at a dot labeled "Mad River Magic's channel."

Bolt studied the map, wanting to remember every detail. The cables lying beside the computers straightened and rose from the tables like slender snakes. The electrodes pressed against the gang's temples, and Bolt felt a soft buzz. He closed his eyes. The map was there! Wonderful.

"Now you see a map of your route," said Omni. "We'll discuss some details soon. But first I want to give you some new tools for your journey."

The carts which had been sitting at the back of the auditorium rose and silently glided to a position beside each member of the gang. A tiny white box appeared on the desk, one for each of them.

"This is your Omni Radio," said Omni. "I know that Solia gave you an Omni Box, but this radio has more power and a much larger range. In fact, it might even survive the return trip to earth. You will discover many uses for it as you explore on your journey. The main thing to know is that you can use it to communicate with me, anytime. Its power source is endless. No batteries required."

Bolt felt his pocket for the Omni Box. It was gone.

"Yes, Bolt," said Omni, "it is gone. I have given you an upgrade. Now put the Omni Radio underneath the dashboard of your cart."

Scout helped each member position and attach their radio.

Next, another strange object appeared in front of them. This device looked like a nozzle for a garden hose, the type that you squeezed to turn on, and could adjust from a fine spray to a focused stream by squeezing harder. It reminded Bolt of the water fights they had at Cedar Heights.

"This is a faze light," said Omni. "Pick it up and try it out."

The gang picked up their new weapon and squeezed. A bright light emanated from the tip, going from a wide fan pattern to a focused beam as they squeezed harder. Bug aimed her light at Bolt. He was instantly paralyzed and dropped to the floor.

"Okay, Bug," said Omni. "I see you have figured out what it does. But don't use it on each other."

Bolt got back up and glared at Bug.

Omni continued. "This faze light will immobilize your enemies. Like the white magic your grandfather taught you, it is to be used defensively for good, never for evil. Keep it in your pocket along with your own wand. It will not survive the time channel back to earth, but will continue to work while you are here in the Strata."

Mad River Magic pocketed the faze light. Bolt glanced at Bug, and could tell she was anxious to use it.

"I will give each of you one more very potent power source," said Omni, "but we'll wait until you are ready to leave. Now for some instructions. You saw the map. Look at it in your mind frequently. Never leave the narrow road. Use your Omni Radio to call in frequently for advice. Your fazer light is for good and for defense only, but use it quickly before your enemies—and they will be many—get too close. Work as a team. You each have useful talents, and working together you are more likely to succeed. So stay together. And finally, remain confident. I have promised you that you can succeed. You need only remember my promise and never doubt that it is true. When doubt creeps in, call me on your radio."

Bolt contemplated the advice. So much to remember. Staying here was sounding better all the time.

"Now, finally, for some warnings," said Omni. "I told you that Contra is my son, but he is not to be trusted. You already have witnessed that with the theft of your cart. He will suspect that I have given you power, and he will try to coerce you into helping him attack Extor. His help will be tempting, but don't take it."

Bolt and Rey looked at each other. Was she ready and up to the challenge? She'd better be.

"Extor will continue to get stronger," said Omni. "If you reflect, his resistance has been escalating. He will be even more dangerous and will stop at nothing to defeat you. Somehow he will know that losing to you will weaken him and make him more vulnerable to Contra or me. He will play on your good intentions and mercy to trick you into doing what he wants. Don't trust him for a second. He'll put many traps in your way.

"One last thought. Taking Finkelstein with you will make this whole process ten times more dangerous. You don't have to do it. It is okay to skip that part. I will protect him here if he doesn't bend to Extor."

Bolt took a deep sigh. Man, this was scary. Could they do it?

"Yes, Bolt," answered Omni, "you can do it. I will give you a power source, just before you leave, that will amaze you. Now it is time for you to rest and reflect. Anna will meet you at the front door and escort you back to your house. I will meet you tomorrow morning at the gate to the city to send you off and to empower you."

Bolt felt a warm sensation under his right arm. He lifted his arm to look, noticing that the rest of the gang was looking, too. On the inner aspect, just below his arm pit, the skin was white with a three-tongue flame shape. Just like the emblem on Benecia's cape. What?

"One more thing," said Omni. "That mark tells the world that you are mine. They cannot control you or harm you. It is your fire bloom, your shield. Wear it with pride."

Chapter Twenty-Five

Father Angel's Advice

*B*olt followed Anna and the gang back to their house, as thoughts jumbled through his mind. Questions had no answers. Why was this so hard? Should they just stay here? And then his mother popped into his mind. No, they couldn't. They had to return. But should they take the risk of rescuing Finkelstein? Omni said they didn't need to, that he would protect Finkelstein, and this was certainly a better place than earth.

He glanced at his cart and remembered the Omni Radio. Could he actually talk to Omni for advice? He hastened his steps and caught up with Anna. He would try to communicate with his father again.

When Mad River Magic reached their house, he hurried back to his bedroom. His father's picture stood on the dresser. The holographic angel was gone, but the last communication remained on the mirror. He read it again, "I'm proud of you son..." A tear formed in Bolt's eye, and he wiped it away quickly.

He began tapping the picture again, and the angel appeared. Good, Bolt had some questions for him.

"Is it really necessary for us to return to earth?" began Bolt. "Or should we stay here with Omni?"

A new message appeared on the mirror. "What you are doing is not for yourself. Remember your mother."

Bolt hung his head. "Is it really necessary to rescue Finkelstein? Omni said he would take care of him."

Another message scrolled onto the mirror. "Just as your mother needs you, Mrs. Finkelstein needs her husband."

Guilt swept over him. Could he do this?

A third message appeared. "I can hear your thoughts, my son. I am proud of you. As Omni promised, you can succeed. He has a surprise gift for you tomorrow that will totally amaze you with its power.

"And one more thing, when you return to earth, you will become your mother's guardian angel. Protect her. She needs you. I must go now. I have other people to help, but I will be watching your progress.

"Oh, I almost forgot. Tell your mother to look inside my old foot locker that's buried in the back of the attic. And do it when Jack isn't around."

"Dad," said Bolt.

But the angel had disappeared. The message faded from the mirror.

Bolt began tapping the picture, but it didn't change. He looked at his young father. "Why did you have to go, Dad?" Oh, he needed him. Yeah, Bolt slapped his forehead, just like his mother needed him.

He lay back on the bed, eyes closed, studying the map and reviewing Omni's instructions.

As Bolt drifted off to sleep, his anxiety and lack of confidence flooded in to fill his dreams.

He found himself outside Omni's mountain, leading Mad River Magic down a narrow dark path through the Hemlock Forest. The turbo-levitators would not function in the forest, and the carts seemed to creep along at a snail's pace.

Chattering and chirping surrounded them. The noise reminded him of the ringracs, and it seemed to be getting closer. Bolt could hear Simi laughing. He could see him pointing his knife and taunting him, "The next time you will be mine."

Why wouldn't the carts move faster? Why wasn't the rest of the gang as worried as he was? Bolt wanted to get out of the cart and push it.

Screams from behind told him that his worst fears were coming true. Turning, he saw Lil and Bug captured, the ringracs sitting on top of the girls and driving their carts. He knew he had to get out and rescue them. But, before he could try, he felt a thump on his cart, and Simi had captured him.

With a knife to Bolt's chest, Simi instructed him to turn down a side path. Heart pounding, sweat dropping from his forehead, Bolt did as instructed. He was helpless to fight back. The rest of the gang followed, a ringrac on each cart to ensure compliance, and the rest of Simi's army of ringracs swarmed around the carts.

A bright fire appeared at the end of the dark forest path. As the gang and the army of ringracs pulled into the clearing where the large fire roared, Bolt could see circular racks hanging from the trees, waiting for their victims. Beside the fire, a long table had been set, ready for a meal to be served.

Mad River Magic was pulled one at a time from their carts and placed on the upside down vertical racks, everyone except Bolt. Simi and three other ringracs carried him to a large spit positioned beside the fire. Bolt struggled, but was helpless against four ringracs. They tied him to the horizontal rotisserie, and then the ringracs stood back. Simi laughed loudly as he sharpened his knife.

When Simi came towards him with the knife, Bolt screamed and twisted, trying to escape.

Thud. Bolt awoke to find himself on the floor beside his bed in his bedroom on Omni's mountain. He pulled himself to his feet, wiping the sweat from his face. His rapid heart rate gradually slowed. He let out a deep sigh. Could Mad River Magic really succeed? Was he capable of leading the gang?

Bolt sat on the side of the bed, head in his hands. Why him? Why couldn't there be someone else to lead, someone older and stronger?

A light flashed on over his dresser. Had his father returned to reassure him, to give him more advice? He hobbled over to the dresser.

A white light glowed from a small cloud over his mirror. On the mirror an invisible finger wrote, "Bolt, it is me, Omni. Why are you unable to sleep?"

Bolt rubbed his eyes and read the message again. "I'm not sure I can do this, Omni. Look at me, weak legs and crutches. Isn't there someone else who could lead us back to our world? Maybe Turtoro, or one of your angels."

A new message scrolled across the mirror. "My son, all leaders question their capabilities at some time or other. What you are experiencing is normal. I have given you the tools you need to succeed. And I promised you that tomorrow I will fill you with a power so awesome you will be totally amazed. Most importantly, you have a heart that is brave and true, the characteristics I am most impressed with."

"But, Omni," Bolt protested.

A new message appeared. "Sleep in the confidence I have promised you. I can read the future, and you will succeed. Now get some rest."

The glowing cloud disappeared, and in spite of many more questions from Bolt, it did not reappear.

Bolt returned to bed and fell into a sound sleep.

Chapter Twenty-Six

Return to Dark Evil

The next thing Bolt knew, the alarm was ringing, and Anna was telling them to get up.

After breakfast, the gang set out for the gate to Omni's Mountain. Lil was clinging to Anna. Rey was directing the carts. Bug was running and singing. Bolt hated to admit that she had found a new talent. Hopefully she would turn down the volume. And as usual, Scout was exploring everything. He certainly would miss this place.

As they walked down the golden street, a crowd was gathering. What was going on up ahead? When they reached the pearly gate, the crowd was large. A bright white cloud hovered over the entire gathering. With his glasses on, Bolt could just barely make out the elderly white-haired Omni within the cloud.

Omni's voice filled the air. "Good morning, my friends. We have gathered to see you off and to wish you a successful journey. As I promised yesterday, I have a surprise for each of you."

The white cloud became even brighter, then extended all the way to the ground. It coalesced into a large three-tongued fire bloom. Each petal was inscribed with a letter "C."

Omni then descended from the cloud and stood beside the gang. "The fire bloom that you wear on your arm is a symbol of something very real, something that I will give you today, something that will make you invincible. Notice that each petal is inscribed with the letter C. Three C's. Courage, confidence, and consistency. You will find the courage to take on every conflict you encounter. You will have the confidence that, with my help, you can overcome every obstacle. And you will forge on with consistency that will take you to your goal."

Omni hugged each member in turn. Then, reaching out to the giant fire bloom, he transported a flickering, living, flame on his finger tip and placed it on each member's heart.

When Omni reached Bolt, he whispered in his ear, "Stay in touch, and we shall lead together."

When Omni transported the flame to Bolt's chest, he felt a rush of power explode within him. Looking at the rest of the gang, he saw them standing straight and proud, their faces glowing with Omni's power. Wow! They were ready.

Mad River Magic mounted their carts and flew single-file out the gate, as the crowd waved and cheered. Omni music filled the air. Anna waved, with tears in her eyes. They were on their way.

The gate closed behind them, and Bolt took the lead. Although light shone from the mountain, the music and the cheering had gone silent, and they found themselves in a thick cloud. Bracing himself for the descent, Bolt called to the rest of the gang, "Roller coaster time!"

The carts, no longer operational at this high altitude, swooped down the mountain in a steep dive. Rather than displaying fear, the gang whooped and hollered, while Scout maintained a tight grip on his steering wheel.

They came out of the clouds, and the narrow road appeared below them. Regaining power, the carts leveled out and flew a few feet above the road. Yes, they were on their way home. But first they would invade Extor's Palace to rescue Finkelstein. They could do this!

In the silent flight, Bolt heard a quiet humming from his dashboard. He looked back and saw that Scout had his ear to the dash. Bolt circled around and flew beside Scout.

"It's the Omni Radio," called Scout. "It sounds like the music we heard on the mountain."

"Yeah," yelled Bug, "and I can hear Omni singing along." She began a loud rendition of what she was hearing.

"Quiet, Bug," said Rey. "Let's enjoy the peacefulness of this place."

Bug wagged her head at Rey and sang silently with exaggerated facial movements and waving of her arms.

Lil shook her head and smiled in amusement.

The joy and excitement ended when they hit the Hemlock Forest. Once again their carts sputtered and dropped to the narrow winding road, but continued rolling. As the trees became larger and grew closer together, the road became shaded and dark. The shiny needles on the trees seemed to flicker back and forth between black and white. An aura of captivity, almost a feeling of something reaching out to strangle them, emanated from the sinister trees. Bolt looked around carefully for ringracs.

He did notice that Omni's Radio continued playing. Putting his ear to the dash, he heard Omni's voice. "Ahead, you will encounter a road block and danger. Keep your faze light on ready, and allow me to help you with the negotiating."

Bolt yelled over his shoulder to the gang, "Get your faze lights out. Be ready for trouble, and keep listening to your Omni Radio."

As they crested the next hill, Bolt saw the catastrophe that Omni had predicted.

"Flying V!" he shouted.

Mad River Magic lined up in a wedge formation and rolled slowly forward, their faze lights held at ready.

Bolt tucked his head down to the dash, listening to Omni.

"Clue. Ringracs are afraid of water," said Omni.

Hmm. Ahead of the gang, at the bottom of the hill, a long narrow bridge crossed a wide river. And in front of the bridge stood a mass of ringracs. Simi stood in the center, on the bridge, blocking the gang's way. On either side of the bridge a line of ringracs stretched out, positioned along the river.

Mad River Magic rolled to a stop thirty feet from the bridge. Simi stepped forward and leered at them.

"We meet again, my succulent friends," growled Simi. "Only this time we are prepared for you." He pointed to the bank of the river where a camp fire was burning and a spit had been built over the fire. A large slab of logs was bound together beside the fire like a giant chopping block. "I believe everything is ready. We need only the ingredients for our meal. Now, who wishes to be the appetizer?"

Bolt stepped out of his cart and stick-hopped toward Simi, faze light on ready.

"What do you propose to do with that toy?" asked Simi. He turned to his soldiers. "Take him."

Bolt pointed his light at one of his crutches, and the reflection on the aluminum sprayed a fan of light that reached to thirty feet on either side of the bridge. The ringracs dropped like dominoes. Bolt grabbed Simi and tossed him over the side of the bridge and into the river. He jumped on top of Simi, jabbing one crutch into the bottom of the river to keep Simi from floating downstream.

"Get the carts across the bridge," yelled Bolt to Rey.

While Rey led the carts and gang across the bridge, he pulled out his other wand and pointed it at the huge chopping block. "*Hakwichinwi!*[25]" commanded Bolt.

The large slab floated out into the river. Bolt positioned himself to keep it from moving down stream and tossed the limp Simi on the raft. "*Wiiwiil'shkwa!*[26]" he yelled. A layer of adhesive oozed out from beneath Simi, cementing him to the raft.

---

[25] Float it! (hah-kwee-chee-nwee)

[26] Glue! (weee-weeel-shkwah)

By now a row of ringracs lined the shore, chirping and squawking, jumping up and down in anger. But none entered the water.

Bolt sprayed the front row of onlookers with his faze light and dragged them, one at a time, to the raft. *"Wiiwiil'shkwa!"* he repeated as he covered the wood with a layer of ringracs.

By now the gang was safely across the bridge, and had returned to help Bolt.

Yelling to Rey, Bolt instructed her to take out a ten-foot section of the bridge.

"Chaakatethilo!" [27] commanded Rey, pointing at the bridge with her wand. She swept it back and forth until a ten-foot section burst into flame and dropped into the river.

Bug eagerly jumped into the fray beside Bolt, zapping ringracs and pulling them onto the raft. "Now we shall eat you, you ugly monsters," she sang as she glued each one to the overflowing barge.

Lil and Scout zapped while Bolt and Bug glued ringracs.

Finally, the remaining ringracs saw what was happening and retreated to a safe distance. The gang then pulled the barge into the current of the river, guided it through the opening in the bridge, and shoved it down stream. The ringracs on the gigantic chopping block began to squirm and growl as the paralysis wore off. The remaining ringracs ran along the edge of the river, following the raft, chattering, but not daring to enter the water.

Mad River Magic climbed out of the water and onto the far section of the bridge. Elated with success, they clapped and cheered and gave each other high fives.

Bolt leaned over the dashboard of his cart and said, "Thank you, Omni."

"Let me guide you into battle," answered Omni, "and you will win."

The gang dried out clothing and resumed their journey, now certain of success.

As they lined up and Bolt prepared to lead, he turned around to the gang. "Thank Omni for that one."

The carts rolled forward, and they were on their way again. Yes, Bolt now had full confidence that they could do this.

As they reached the edge of the Hemlock Forest, the boredom of slow progress began to set in. The trees thinned, the air warmed up. Bolt could see the desert ahead.

"Come on carts," he said. "Time for lift off again."

But the carts would not fly.

"Hey, look over there," yelled Scout, pointing to the right.

A small trail left the road and wound into the edge of the forest. Camouflaged behind the trees, a large cave entrance blended into the landscape.

---

[27] Burn up! (chaah-kah-tay-thee-lo)

Bolt closed his eyes, looking at the map. "Ah, yes, that is Contra's Cavern. Everyone stay quiet until we get past." He leaned toward the dash, to hear Omni's voice.

"They're coming," said Omni. "Get your faze lights ready, and do *not* get out of your carts, no matter what Contra tells you. Let me do the negotiating."

A gray blur flashed in front of Bolt and dropped onto the road. It was Contra, followed by his shape-shifting ghosts.

Bolt stopped his cart, hand on his faze light.

"Good day, my cart friends," said Contra, gliding toward Bolt's cart.

"Stay back," said Bolt, pointing his faze light.

"I see you have been to Omni's Mountain," said Contra. "What other gadgets did he give you?"

Bolt remained silent listening to his radio.

"Apparently Omni didn't find the bug I placed in the carts," said Contra. "Have you noticed the carts won't fly over the desert like they did before?"

Bolt did not answer.

"Didn't Omni teach you to be civil to your friends?" asked Contra, edging closer.

"Get back," said Bolt. "He told me that you were not to be trusted."

Bolt waved his faze light, keeping his eyes on Contra and his ghosts.

"Come, come," said Contra, with a forced smile. "If you get out of your carts, I will fix them. And you can be on your way."

Contra's ghosts began to surround the gang.

"Omni told us to stay in our carts," said Bolt. "So if you will kindly step aside, we will be on our way and will not trouble you."

The ghosts burst into laughter, rolling and spinning in the air as they held their sides. Contra held up a gray draped arm, and the laughter ceased immediately.

"We will not let you pass, until you relinquish your carts," said Contra. The smile on his gray face, had turned into a sneer. "Where are you going? Is this a mission for Omni?"

Bolt ducked his head to the radio.

Omni's voice became louder. "I will negotiate with Contra." And suddenly the air was filled with Omni's deep booming voice. "Contra, my prodigal son. If you will not hinder my friends and will allow them to pass, I will ground Extor's winged wolves for twenty-four hours."

"How do I know that voice is really you?" asked Contra, rubbing his dirty translucent chin that jutted out from his dark gray hood.

Omni's voice spoke into Bolt's ears, and apparently the rest of the gang. "Show Contra your fire bloom."

Mad River Magic held up their arms in unison, revealing their white brands.

Contra's ghosts recoiled, moving back and whispering to each other.

"Okay," said Contra. "When does this twenty-four-hour period begin?"

"Now," said Omni.

"How about letting it start when we arrive at Extor's palace?"

"You're wasting time," said Omni. "It starts right now."

Contra swirled around his ghosts. The mass of ghosts swarmed into the air like a tornado of gray hornets and zipped over the Desert of Indecision. They were gone in a flash.

The gang looked around in surprise.

"Thank you, Omni," said Lil.

"Yeah, thanks," said the rest of the gang.

Omni's voice became quiet again, with music in the background. "You are welcome, my friends. Continue listening to me and following my advice, and you will succeed."

Suddenly the carts lifted off and sped forward above the narrow road, skirting the Desert of Indecision. As the gang cheered, Bolt looked back at the entrance to Contra's Cavern. He didn't see any more ghosts, but something told him that Contra would not keep his end of the bargain.

Mad River Magic had barely traveled a few minutes when they came to a Y in the road. The narrow road they had followed continued straight and skirted the desert. The wide road turned and wound in the direction Contra's ghosts had taken. Bolt closed his eyes and looked at the map. This road wasn't on the map.

Now what? The larger road appeared to be a shorter route to Extor's Palace of Night. Should they take it? He put his ear to the dashboard and listened for Omni's voice.

"Fly high and look at the big picture," said Omni.

Bolt led the gang into a high altitude flight. Looking ahead he could see the narrow road skirting the desert, while the wider road wandered through the desert. In the distance Bolt could see a glowing gray speck. Extor's palace. He compared the two routes. The wide road would definitely get them to Extor's Palace quicker, and he definitely wanted to get there while the wolves were grounded and Contra was creating havoc.

"Come on," said Bolt. "Let's take this route."

"I thought Omni told us to stay on the narrow road," said Rey.

"He did," said Bolt. "But he also told us to take a look at the big picture."

"Why don't we ask—" said Scout.

"Come on," yelled Bolt as he sped down the wide road. "Let's get there while all the commotion is going on."

Bug slapped her hands together. "Let's do it."

Rey shook her head as if questioning the decision.

It quickly became obvious what the risks of this route were. For as the carts moved over the desert, the air became warm, then hot. Perspiration dripped from Bolt's face. He turned to check on the rest of the gang. They were wiping sweat off their faces as well.

"Let's find some shade," called Rey.

"Yeah, there are some trees over there." Bug pointed at what appeared to be an oasis sitting off the road in the distance.

"Omni said to stay on the road," said Lil.

"Lil's right," said Bolt. "Let's keep moving. Maybe we'll find some shade beside the road."

"Look," shouted Scout, pointing. "There are some trees ahead."

When they reached the trees, they were beside the road. The shade looked cool, and the gang jumped out of their carts. Rey and Lil lay down to take a nap. Bolt stretched his legs, looking around in the wilderness. Something about this place just wasn't right.

Bug had ventured farther away from the road. "Hey, there's a little spring of water out here," she shouted. Does anyone want a drink?"

Rey yawned without opening her eyes. "Yeah, bring me a drink."

"Wait," shouted Scout, who had remained beside the road. "That water's probably contaminated. Don't touch it, Bug."

"Then come test it," Bug replied.

Scout reluctantly ventured out to the spring and pulled out his wand. After dipping the tip into the water, he announced, "Ten parts per million of contraband."

"Well, what's that?" asked Bug.

"I have no idea," answered Scout. "But I wouldn't drink it."

"Probably contamination from Contra's cavern," said Bolt, with a chuckle.

"Let's ask Omni," said Rey, stretching and hopping into her cart. After listening for a few minutes, she lifted her head. "Omni said we're following the wrong road, but he told me how to treat the water."

She marched to the spring and stretched out Omni's faze light. "Clarify!" she commanded.

A burst of white light jumped from the fazer into the water. The faint gray tinge to the water disappeared, and the water glistened clear.

Rey scooped up a handful and drank. "The best water I've ever tasted."

The rest of the gang quenched their thirst.

"Come on," said Bolt. "We better get moving."

"Let's take a quick nap first," mumbled Rey, yawning and heading back to her cart.

Bolt splashed water on her. "I think Omni provided this water to wash away your indecision. Now let's get going."

Rey seemed to become more alert. "Well, what about the fact that we're on the wrong road?"

"We've already established that this route is the quicker way to get to Extor's palace," said Bolt. "Let's keep going."

As the carts moved out again, Lil muttered, "Shouldn't we ask Omni? But then, who's listening to me?"

Bolt looked out at the expanse of the desert ahead. Why follow any road? Let's just fly straight to Extor's palace. He moved higher above the desert where he could see the speck in the distance, then set out on a straight line for his destination.

But the going was slow. Hot currents off the desert below forced him to constantly change altitude. The gang repeatedly asked for breaks to find shade. Rey wanted to take naps. And then there were the huge black birds.

The first time, Scout shouted a warning. Bolt saw a strange dark cloud heading their way. He took the gang down to the desert and they camouflaged themselves in the gray sand with gray sheets. The cloud of dark blurs became a huge swarming flock of vulture-like creatures that were bigger than eagles. They landed in nearby trees, bending them nearly to the ground with their weight, while they squawked and cackled. Their sight must not have been too good, because they never moved toward the gang. After about an hour, the flock moved on.

"What were those?" asked Scout, as they resumed their flight.

"I have no idea," answered Bolt. "But let's get out of here."

"I'm going to ask Omni," said Lil. She put her head close to the dashboard. "Omni said they're call extures, and they have excellent vision. He also said that we're still on the wrong road, and beware of wheel grabbers."

"What's a wheel grabber?" asked Bolt anxiously looking ahead. "I'm sorry, but we're not going to turn around now. We're almost there, and we better hurry if we're going to get there before that twenty-four hours is up."

The second time Mad River Magic saw the extures, Bolt could tell that trouble was coming. The first group must have been a scouting party. This group knew where the gang was, and they were coming in fast. A line of black dots stretched across the horizon like a wave of fighter jets. Bolt knew there was no sense in trying to hide.

"Come on, gang," yelled Bolt, as he spun around and headed in the opposite direction. "Full throttle."

He lead Mad River Magic in a bee line back toward the forest. Bolt's mind was racing. Where would they hide? What spell could they use to take on a hundred black ugly birds?

He put his head down to the dashboard. "What do we do, Omni? An army of extures is closing in on us. Wow, they're fast."

Omni's calm voice was clear. "What hiding place did I just empty?"

The rest of the gang must have been listening. Scout looked at Bolt, then pointed at the edge of the forest and the trail that led to Contra's cavern.

Bolt put his head down again. "Contra's cavern?"

"Bingo." Omni laughed. "I'll have the lights on for you. And don't stop when you get inside. Just follow the lights."

Bolt wasn't sure what that meant, but he was glad to have a plan. He glanced back. Yes, they could make it to the cavern before the extures caught up with them.

The gang entered the single entrance to the cave. Bolt had slowed slightly. He wasn't brave enough to hit that dark hole at full speed. Beside the six-foot entrance, sat a large gray boulder. He wouldn't want to be trapped behind that monster.

Like a single file line of bees entering the hive, Mad River Magic zipped in behind Bolt. Lanterns burned brightly on the walls. As Bolt looked for the path, the lanterns began lighting in the distance, flashing one after another, pointing the way. Bolt cranked up his speed and followed.

Looking back to make sure everyone was following, Bolt noticed the lanterns behind them had gone dark. He also noticed the first of the extures were hot on their tail, and they didn't seem to be afraid of the dark. Bolt called to the gang to crank up their speed.

Omni and the flashing lights led them on a tour deep into the cavern. The faster the gang flew, the farther ahead of them the lights flashed. They were putting some distance between themselves and the extures. Through eating chambers and sleeping rooms, storage spaces and passageways, Mad River Magic zipped down one tunnel after another.

Bolt continued to think, trying to come up with a way to put a sudden obstacle in the path of their pursuers. But there were no doors, no sliding walls, nothing that could be quickly moved. What did Omni have planned? Was there a side passage the gang could duck into until the birds passed? He saw nothing.

"Omni, where are you taking us?" asked Bolt, leaning into the dashboard, and getting more nervous by the second.

"Just follow the flashing white lights," came Omni's response.

Bolt glanced back again. The entire gang was following, trusting him to lead. They didn't really have a choice. Why did he struggle with trusting Omni to lead? It seemed like he still had to make a choice, make a decision. Oh, get us out of here alive, Omni.

"Hang on to your cart, Bolt," came Omni's reply. "We're going to put some distance between the gang and that ugly dark flock."

The rest of the gang must have heard the conversation. In the next second their carts blasted ahead at twice the speed, sliding around corners, taking dives down inclines, and climbing vertically up ventilation shafts. Before they could take their white-knuckled hands off the steering wheels, they were back at the entrance and erupting into the light outside the cavern.

Their carts skidded to a stop on the ground and spun to face the entrance.

"Get out," instructed Omni, "and roll the stone in front of the opening."

Bolt grabbed his crutches and stick hopped to the boulder. How were they going to move this monster? "Come on, gang," he yelled.

Mad River Magic lined up and pushed and strained. At first the boulder didn't budge, then it began slowly rolling. The gang continued to strain, and the boulder rolled faster, then came to a stop in front of the entrance. Bolt glanced up at a flash of light and saw Tutoro smile at him, then disappear into a white meteor that sped toward Omni's mountain.

Bolt shook his head in amazement. The gang cheered and gave each other high fives.

The joy and confidence subsided quickly when the sound of extures on the other side of the boulder reminded them that danger was always around the corner. Scout looked up to see if any birds were exiting ventilation shafts. Rey was studying her map. Bug was slapping the rock and taunting the extures. Lil was wringing her hands and encouraging the gang to get moving. She wanted to go home.

Yes, they could do this. Bolt's confidence grew. They had lost time in escaping the extures. They needed to make up for that lost time and take the most direct route to Extor's palace. They would follow Contra's path and head directly across the desert.

The lighter hours were beginning to dim, and the twenty-four hours were almost over when the gang reached the perimeter of Extor's Palace of Night.

The wide road wound back and forth beneath them again, and Bolt led the gang down. "We'll be less likely to draw attention here," he said. "Watch for a large tunnel under the wall. My map says it's a ventilation shaft. Should be a good place to hide our carts and gain access to the courtyard."

Mad River Magic rolled along the road, studying the wall. The dark hours were getting darker. Bolt glanced nervously overhead. Still no flying wolves. Maybe they would make it.

A rattling sound brought Bolt's attention back to the road. Glancing down, he saw that they were rolling across a cattle-guard-like box with rails. As he looked over the side of his cart in disbelief, chains reared their ugly heads like cobras. They coiled and struck, wrapping themselves around his tires and jolting him to a sudden stop.

Screams from the rest of the gang told him that all the carts had been captured. Looking over the side of his cart, Bolt inspected the chains and saw that they were fastened to the box below. These chains weren't going to let them go anywhere.

"Get those snakes off me," screamed Rey. She stood on her seat with her arms held tight to her chest, ready to jump.

"Those are chains, not snakes," said Scout. "Sit down and stay in your cart."

Bolt leaned over and listened to his Omni Radio. It was quiet. "Come on, Omni. We need you."

Silence.

Bolt pulled out his wand. "*Pkwahilo!*[28]" he commanded, pointing at the chains. The chains remained.

Bug aimed her faze light at the chains. "Let go, you serpentine parasites." Nothing happened.

"Do you have the plasma cutter?" Bolt asked Scout.

"I left it at Solia's palace," he answered.

Bolt banged his forehead on his steering wheel. What now? Were they being punished for not following the narrow road? Did Omni's powers not extend into Extor's territories?

He leaned over the dash. "I'm sorry, Omni," he said. "Don't leave us now."

A quiet voice came from the radio. "I have not left you, and never will. I cannot change the consequences of your disobedience. You will have to proceed on foot. Take your radios and lights with you. You can still succeed...if you listen to me."

A tear formed in Bolt's eye, but determination burned within. He glanced at Rey and saw her listening to her radio. He nodded at her. Yes, their leading would now be a triangle with Omni at the front.

"Okay, gang," said Bolt. "Omni says we should proceed on foot. Take your radio, your faze light, and your wands with you."

Mad River Magic jumped out of their carts, and Bolt stick-hopped, leading the way. The light was almost gone, and they hadn't found the ventilation shaft yet.

---

[28] Break off! (pkwah-hee-lo)

Chapter Twenty-Seven

In Line for the Recycling Plant

A flapping of wings and a sudden stench in the air made the gang whirl and look up, but it was too late. The extures were already on them. Bolt dropped into a fetal position, curled up like a baby, defenseless. He felt the claws surround his arms. He managed to hang onto his crutches as he was lifted into the air.

He turned to the screaming and saw the rest of the gang suspended beneath the ugly birds. Mad River Magic was lifted up and over the wall as the birds flapped like large stinky eagles bearing their prizes to be plopped down into Extor's courtyard.

The scene before him revealed extreme chaos. The last glimpses of gray flashes disappeared into the night as Contra and his ghosts retreated. The ground of the courtyard was littered with gray stratoids, wounded in battle, becoming fainter and fainter as they stopped moving. Windows in the palace walls shone with gray light and displayed the damage Contra had inflicted. Glass was broken, bars were bent. Holes punched openings in the wall like swiss cheese.

And over the entire mess, Extor was floating back and forth, yelling and screaming and shaking his claw-like fists. "Where are the wolves? Where are the wolves?"

The extures set down the gang in the middle of the courtyard, claws tightly fastened, waiting for Extor. As his fury gradually dissipated, he fluttered to the giant birds of prey and their captured prisoners.

Recognition flamed in Extor's eyes, the gray light flickered yellow and red, then returned to gray. "What have we here?" he asked the extures.

A raspy voice over Bolt's head was accompanied by the putrid smell of rotting flesh. "We found these creatures slinking around outside the wall, Master. We thought you might want to know."

"Good work, Carotus," said Extor. "My men will take them from here."

A ring of large dark-gray stratoids surrounded the gang, as the extures flew up and over the building and disappeared into the darkness.

"So, my fickle friends, you have returned," said Extor. "Were you part of Contra's attack? I did not see you earlier in the thick of the battle. Or were you holding my wolves at bay while Contra wreaked his havoc?" He rubbed his chin with his long fingers and squinted. "Ah, I see from your clothing that you have visited Omni. Was the sacrifice he asked too great? Have you returned to me to learn how to enjoy all the pleasures of the night?"

He raised one hand with an extended pointer finger, as if pausing in discovery. "But wait, you have a price to pay. Let me see." He snapped his fingers and a long list appeared in his hand. "Oh, but the list is long. Would you like me to recite all the damages you have caused?" He scanned down the list. "Or should I just give you the bottom line?"

Extor looked up and glared at the gang. "I'm afraid the total adds up to the maximum penalty. You will be recycled. Oh, the essence of your free will should be very valuable indeed. It is not often that we have subjects as determined as you. In fact, we will do some special studies on your juices, I mean your essence."

Extor whirled to go, then stopped and turned around. "I almost forgot. Your good friend and neighbor, Mr. Finkelstein is scheduled for recycling tomorrow. How convenient. I'm certain that when we return your bodies to your *real world*, as you call it, we can find a creative way to arrange the bodies. Should keep the authorities scratching their heads for a long time. Hmm."

He whirled and floated away. Calling over his shoulder, he commanded, "Put them in the cell beside Finkelstein's."

Bolt looked around at the damage, getting his bearings, while the stratoids led Mad River Magic to the holding cells.

Bolt had never learned where the recycling plant was. From their escape and aerial view of Extor's Palace, he knew that the building was sprawling with many wings. He looked at each member of the gang, holding his head up and standing straight, until they had all looked him in the eye. All was not lost. They would find a way. Omni's power would prove to be enough.

At least this solved the problem of finding Finkelstein. Now he just needed to think of a plan for escape.

The burly dark gray stratoids herded Mad River Magic through a door and into a wing of Extor's Palace that Bolt had not noticed before. The hallway was dimly lit, dirty, and smelled of body odor. The walls consisted of vertical bars. The doors were prison doors. And the prisoners in the cells were not enjoying the pleasures that had been present in the reception center. Moans and pleas for help floated into the hallway. Bolt looked ahead, down the hallway. It stretched as far as he could see. The floor was scratched and dusty. Ceiling lights were missing or no longer functioning. And everything was the same depressing dark gray.

Bolt's stomach tightened. How were they going to get out of this?

Glancing again at the gang, he was disappointed to see that they had all hung their heads. Tears streamed down Lil's cheeks. Even Bug displayed no sign of defiance. Scout, however, seemed to be surveying his environment with curiosity. Hopefully he was working on ideas.

After they had walked to the far end of the prison wing, the stratoids stopped and opened a cell door. Bolt looked around. The stench and the dirt was overwhelming, but no moans or sounds of prisoners came from the surrounding cells.

The leader of the stratoids looked at Bolt and laughed. "Not as noisy down here as it was at the other end, is it? By the time your brave rebels are moved down to this end, the starvation diet and dehydration have concentrated the free will and made it easier for our extraction." He laughed a villain's cackle. "Not much bravado left, is there?"

Bolt stared straight ahead and didn't answer.

"Maybe we can arrange for you to watch as one of your fellow fools is wrung dry of their juices tomorrow," said the stratoid. "You might want to find some ear plugs. Not a pleasant sound."

The entire group of stratoids burst into laughter.

The cell door opened and the gang was pushed inside. The door slammed into place and the key was removed.

As the stratoids marched down the hall, the leader called over his shoulder, "Please don't disturb any of the other prisoner's last night of sleep."

Bolt surveyed their cell. Bare. Two hard benches, one on either side. A drain hole, and...nothing more. No water. No blankets. No toilet. His heart sank.

He walked to the door. Perfectly quiet except for some snores. No guard could be seen. This was the dead end of death row. Tomorrow they would be hauled out and squished.

Bolt sat down on one of the benches beside Scout and hung his head. Reality was setting in. There was nothing they could do.

Lil's voice whispered from the other side of the cell. "We still have our radios. Let's talk to Omni."

Mad River Magic huddled around Bolt and his Omni Radio.

"What now, Omni?" pleaded Bolt. "What can we do? We need your help."

Omni's voice was quiet but strong. "I told you that you would need me. You have more power than you think. I have put Mr. Finkelstein within your reach. The cage truck that will transport you tomorrow will pass close to the portal I have arranged for your travel back to your world. Now it is time for you to use your talents and skills and devise a plan. Remember the three Cs that I have given you."

Then the radio became silent.

The group looked at each other in silence. Despair and fatigue morphed facial expressions into flat lines with drooping heads.

Bolt rubbed the inner aspect of his right arm, feeling the fire bloom. He took a deep breath and felt a warmth in his chest. "Now wait a second," he said. "What are we doing? Where's the courage? Where's the confidence? Where's the consistency to keep-on-going? Let's find that hidden talent and skill Omni mentioned." He looked around the group. "What do we have to lose? Remember the decision we made back when we escaped this place the first time?"

"Yeah," said Bug, jumping up and stomping her foot. "We have more power now than we did then." She pointed at her fire bloom. "We can do this!"

Rey cleared her throat. "Bug is right. We still have all the tools we had when we escaped the first time. If we make our break from the transport truck, like Omni said, we'll have Finkelstein with us. We'll be close to the portal Omni wants us to use."

"And we can rig a gray light into a plasma cutter again," said Scout. "So many of these aren't working." He pointed at the hallway full of unlit lights. "The stratoids won't even notice if we take one."

"What about our carts?" asked Lil in a tearful voice. "I want to take my cart home with me."

Rey put her hand on Lil's shoulder. "I'm going to talk to Omni. Maybe if I plead hard enough, he'll tell me how to unwind those snakes from our wheels."

Bolt looked around at the group until there was a grim smile on each face. He pulled them into a huddle, a team ready to charge onto the field for the championship game. Do or die.

They stacked their hands and whispered a yell, "One, two, three, courage, confidence, consistency!"

Then Mad River Magic went to work on their individual chores.

Bolt turned to Finkelstein's cell. "Mr. Finkelstein, can you hear me?"

A muffled raspy voice answered. "Yes, I can hear you."

"Did you hear our discussion?"

The prisoner in the next cell slowly rolled up onto his side. "I got the gist of it. You'll never succeed."

"Are you willing to go with us if we do succeed?" asked Bolt, slowly and quietly.

"I will," Finkelstein answered, "on one condition."

"And what is that?"

"On the condition, that if taking me will slow you down and decrease your chance of escape, I want to be left behind." Finkelstein paused and drew a slow raspy breath. "I would rather you make it back and take care of my wife, than we all fail."

"It's a deal, sir," said Bolt. He thought of his mother. He would do the same. "Now I have a question for you."

"I'm listening."

Bolt looked at the cell on the other side of theirs. It was empty. "What is the best way to get some tools out of here with us tomorrow?"

Finkelstein was quiet for awhile. "Put them in my pants. The guards grab and sling bodies. They couldn't care less. We're dead trash to them. Squish and discard. Put the tools in my pants leg, and I'll tie off the bottom of my pants."

Bolt thought for a moment. Not a great idea, but he couldn't think of a better one. "We'll have a few things ready before the light hours. Now get some sleep."

He paused and looked at the ceiling where there were two pipes visible, a supply pipe and a drain pipe. He aimed his fazer light at the supply pipe and squeezed. A nick in the pipe allowed a drip, drip, drip of water to fall beside Finkelstein's seat.

"Now get some water and rehydrate," said Bolt. "You'll need it tomorrow."

Chapter Twenty-Eight

Cage Truck Breakout

For once the dark hours were not long enough, but Mad River Magic hurried with their tasks. And by the time the light hours were creeping into the prison, they were ready. There had been no time for sleep.

Mr. Finkelstein struggled to the bars between the two cells, and Bolt placed a package wrapped in a piece of his shirt into Mr. Finkelstein's pants. He handed Finkelstein one of his shoe laces, and the package was secured.

The gang had settled back onto their benches for a few minutes of rest when the clanking began at the far end of hallway.

Deep gruff voices yelled for the prisoners to awake. Metal pans banged on the bars and the prison doors. Prisoners groaned.

Yells of "There's no food on my plate," were followed by laughter from the guards and warnings to "Get used to it."

Sounds of water splashing on the floors of the cells were followed by prisoners scrambling to get a drink from their bowl, then calling, "Please, could I have some more?"

Bolt shuddered as he imagined the scene that was approaching their end of the prison. Lil had her hands over her ears, and her cheeks were wet with tears. The rest of the gang, except Bug, leaned forward as if in prayer. Bug stood on her bench and hung onto the prison bars, anger blazing in her eyes, as she looked in the direction of the torture.

"Please don't say anything, Bug," said Bolt

Teeth clenched, she shook her head and climbed down from the bench, muttering something about paybacks.

The clamor became less noisy as the guards proceeded to their end of the hallway. Prisoners made no response to the taunting. Too weak to crawl to the door and their bowls, they made no request for more water. Eventually the guards stopped rattling the bars, and the only sound was water slopping into the bowls.

Bolt took a deep breath. The end was near.

The guards suddenly turned and headed back down the hall. Silence returned to the prison.

Then the large door in the hallway, outside Finkelstein's cell, rattled and swung open. Gray light flowed into the hallway. Through the door, Bolt could see a cage truck.

He looked back at the gang. "We're on."

The guards opened the door to their cell.

Two burly stratoids in dark gray uniforms strode in. "Okay, humanoids, empty your pockets."

Fear and desperation filled Rey's eyes as they met Bolt's. Each member of the gang emptied their pockets, laying two radios on the bench.

The guards scooped the radios up and dumped them on the floor, then stomped them into tiny pieces.

"Now, I know some of you have magic sticks," said the guard, laughing. "Put your hands in the air."

He proceeded to pat them down, pulling wands from the waists of Lil and Scout.

Turning to Bolt, the guard approached with a sneer on his face. "Under orders from Extor, I am instructed to give you a special inspection." Without warning, the stratoid punched Bolt in the stomach.

The Omni Radio popped out of Bolt's mouth and landed on the floor.

"I thought so," said the guard, smashing the box with his boot.

"Now down on your hands and knees," he commanded, snatching Bolt's crutches and bending them over his knee. He inspected the crutches, then jabbed Bolt in the side rolling him over. Reaching into Bolt's pants, he pulled out a wand.

Standing over Bolt, while Bolt lay on his back, the guard asked. "Anything else you're hiding?"

Bolt was struggling for air, and only shook his head.

"Okay, now get into the truck," commanded the guards.

Bolt struggled to get to his feet without the crutches. The second guard grabbed him by the back of his shirt and carried him to the truck, tossing him into the cage. The rest of the gang followed.

The first guard tossed the mangled crutches on top of Bolt. "Here, don't forget your walking sticks." The two guards choked with laughter.

Watching in horror, Mad River Magic sat helplessly as Finkelstein was carried out of the prison, suspended by his arms and his legs. At the door to the cage truck, the guards switched their grip to Finkelstein's sides and slung him, like a sack of potatoes, into the cage. Bolt dove and caught Finkelstein's head, preventing it from slamming into the floor. The door of the cage truck slammed shut and was locked.

After sauntering to the front of the truck, the guards climbed into the cab. One of them opened the window between the cab and cage. "Any special requests for music, for your final ride." The guards roared with laughter and slid the window closed. Without a sound, the truck moved forward on a blanket of air.

"Are you okay?" asked Bolt, leaning over Finkelstein.

Finkelstein moaned and opened his eyes. "You'll never pull this off," he whispered. "But thank you for trying. And please don't slow down your escape with me. Just make it back to Cedar Heights and take care of my wife."

"We'll see," said Bolt, a determined smile on his face.

He nodded at Bug. She ducked below the window and pulled a wand from her pony tail. Aiming the wand at the back window, she pronounced, "*Hatchi kiishoowenaki!*[29]"

A silver film covered the window between the cab and the cage. A flickering image moved on the inside surface of the screen.

Bolt nodded to Rey. She took her wand from Bug. Then, pointing behind the truck, back toward Extor's Palace, she whispered, "Omnipotence!"

A faint explosion was accompanied by a dust of gray over the top of the palace. A speck appeared in front of the cloud and became quickly larger. Before long the speck was five specks. Then five barrel carts, minus their wheels, flew over the cage truck.

Meanwhile, Bolt quickly opened Finkelstein's pants and pulled out the contraband. He handed off Scout's invention. Pulling out a second package, he unwrapped two Omni Radios and gave one to Rey. He handed each member of the gang their faze light. Finally, he pulled out his wand and placed it in his waist band.

The gang covered their eyes while Scout turned on his plasma cutter and zapped wires, producing a large hole in the top of the cage. Bolt held the piece, preventing it from falling, then set it down gently beside Finkelstein.

While listening with one ear to her Omni Radio, Rey directed the carts to land on top of the truck.

Bug climbed through the opening to turn on the carts and have them ready.

After rolling Finkelstein onto the section of cage removed from the top, Scout and Bolt lifted Finkelstein up through the opening. They then climbed to the top of the truck and welded the metal bed between two of the carts. Finkelstein was positioned as comfortable as was possible with Scout's shirt.

---

[29] Moving pictures (hah-tchee keee-shoo-way-nah-kee)

Finally, Rey pointed her wand at Bolt's mangled crutches. "*Shooshkilo!*[30]" They snapped back to straight, and Bolt fastened them to his cart.

Lil and Rey followed them to the top of the truck. The gang got into their carts and prepared for lift off.

Rey kept her ear to Omni's Radio. Suddenly a large smile brightened her face. "Now!" she announced. "Omni says the portal is within eye sight."

The carts lifted from the top of the truck and banked off to the right. Finkelstein's cot was supported between Lil's and Bug's carts. He opened his eyes briefly, smiled, and shook his head in disbelief.

Bug and Lil leaned over Finkelstein, crossing their faze lights, like swords before a duel, then aimed them back at the recycling center truck. "*Pkale shkote!*[31]" they shouted in unison. A large bonfire burst into flame on top of the truck. And the truck quickly melted down with the wire cage wrapped around a molten mass of plastic cab. The girls then shook hands and yelled once more, "For the prisoners!"

A white flame flickered in the distance. Bolt set course. That had to be the portal. Within minutes, the flickering became a bright white fire bloom. Bolt heaved a sigh of relief.

And then he looked behind the gang.

---

[30] Straighten! (shoosh-kee-lo)
[31] Blazing fire! (pkah-lay-shko-tay)

Chapter Twenty-Nine

Jousting with Extor

ne hundred yards behind Mad River Magic, and closing fast, Extor rode a winged wolf. Fire spewed from the mouth of the wolf. Extor was waving his arms and yelling, "Faster! Faster!"

Bolt looked at the fire bloom, then back at Extor. There was no way the gang would reach the portal before Extor caught them. He took a deep breath, knowing what he had to do.

Bolt turned to Rey. "Head straight for that fire bloom. Don't look back. Don't stop for anything!"

Swinging his cart around the rest of the gang, he yelled at them to stay the course and not look back. Bolt then turned to face Extor. It was time to destroy the monster.

He pulled his wand and his faze light from their hiding places and kept his cart moving. He wasn't going to be a sitting duck. Heart racing, hands sweating, he charged. "Omni help me," he screamed.

Extor was laughing as they zipped past each other, like knights in a jousting match. Bolt zapped the winged wolf. A large hiss of hot air escaped and the wolf dropped toward the ground.

Great! But then Bolt saw a gray lightning flash discharge from Extor's extended finger. Bolt felt a searing vibration spread through his body, and suddenly his cart was dropping, spiraling down beside Extor.

Bolt pointed the faze light at Extor to immobilize him, but felt an Arctic blast of compressed air hiss from Extor's mouth. It knocked Bolt out of the cart. Shivering, he dropped the light. But he managed to hang onto the cart.

As the cart bounced off the plastic surface below, Bolt grabbed his crutches and stood to face his enemy. He pointed his wand at Extor. It was supposed to be for good magic, but this had to be an exception. "*Nimachilota!*[32]" he commanded.

Extor laughed and dodged. The winged wolf behind him heaved and crumpled.

A rod of black light erupted from Extor's other hand. Suddenly Bolt's hand was invisible. His whole arm was numb, as if it weren't attached, and then his wand was gone.

"You fool," yelled Extor. "Do you really think that you can fight me with your toys? You crippled, stick-legged, skinny little wimp. I knew you would find a way to escape the trip to the recycling center. I would have been disappointed if you hadn't. Now I will wring every single drop of free will from your pathetic body. Before I am done with you, you will grovel at my feet and beg forgiveness."

"Never," yelled Bolt. He lifted a crutch and pointed it at Extor.

Extor reached down and pulled on the plastic floor. Like a rug being pulled from beneath him, Bolt felt the ground move. His legs flew forward. He fell backwards. His crutches bounced into the air.

Bolt twisted to grab the crutches, but two long scrawny hands swept over him and slammed the crutches out of reach.

Now Bolt was on his back and Extor was above him. It was over. He tried to look around Extor to see if the gang had reached the portal, but Extor's black toga was in the way. A lump in his back pocket reminded him that he still had his radio.

"Help me, Omni," whispered Bolt.

Extor stopped, hands outstretched for Bolt's neck. He roared with laughter. "And how will Omni help you? Do you have him on speed dial? Will he give you wings?"

Bolt twisted with a kick, thrusting his weak left leg into Extor's face.

Extor spun away and grabbed Bolt's leg. "Thank you. Now the fun begins."

A vice-like grip clamped down on his leg as Extor began twisting. The stench of Extor's breath added to the excruciating pain. Bolt tried to kick with his other leg. Extor grabbed it and began crunching it, also.

The pain in his legs ratcheted up and up. Bolt fought to keep the tears from his eyes. He would never bow to this monster. Never! Even if he died.

"Are you ready to grovel and plead for mercy, Stick Leg?" Extor squeezed and twisted harder.

Bolt heard a faint voice from behind him. "You have my power within you, Bolt."

Bolt raised his head from the plastic and screamed at Extor. "I will never grovel before you. By the pow—"

Extor was on top of him, his fetid breath in Bolt's face. His voice raged in Bolt's ears.

---

[32] I destroy it! (nee-mah-chee-lo-tah)

"You have no power except what I grant you. And I will now wring you dry of every last drop."

Extor reared back and opened his mouth, revealing dagger-like fangs. His arms reached for Bolt's neck.

In that instant, Bolt grabbed his shirt and tore it open. "By Omni's power!"

A blinding explosion of sunshine burst from Bolt's chest. The golden light radiated through Extor, immobilizing him. A horrified look froze on his face, and he began to fade. The gray of his body and the black of his robe began to float down like dark gray snowflakes. Then the flakes fizzled into a heap of ashes. The pain in Bolt's legs disappeared. And the sweet smell of clean air displaced the stench.

Bolt rolled over to look for his crutches and found them tapping the floor beside him.

"Are you looking for these?" It was the deep resonate voice of Omni, who was standing beside Bolt. He handed Bolt his crutches and his wand.

Bolt pulled himself up to standing, then shielded his eyes from the light. "Thank you, Omni."

"I told you I would help you fight your battles if you would listen to me," said Omni. "Are you hurt?"

Bolt rubbed his legs. "I don't think so." He looked around for the gang. They were gone, and the fire bloom was no longer visible. "Did they make it back?" Bolt pointed in the direction of the portal.

"They did," answered Omni. "And Mr. Finkelstein made it back, too. Thanks to you."

"What will happen with me now?" asked Bolt. What would his mother think when she saw the gang, and he wasn't with them. A tear formed in his eye.

"You still long for home, don't you?" said Omni, smiling at Bolt. "It's not too late to choose to stay on my mountain. You are always welcome there."

"I want to go home..." Bolt paused, "if there is a way." He looked expectantly at Omni. Was it possible?

"Come with me, my son," said Omni. He began to float toward the location of the fire bloom.

"But my cart does not work," said Bolt.

"Have faith, my son." A beam of light shone from Omni's face to Bolt's cart.

The cart hovered and sidled up to Bolt. Bolt got in and pinched himself. Yes, he was alive.

Bolt placed the radio under the dash, attached his crutches, and hurried to catch up with Omni. Yes, this was really happening.

By the time he reached Omni, they were under the giant fire bloom. Wow, a ten-foot base hovered in mid-air. The petals waved upward, burning with white fire, but not being consumed. The bright light nearly blinded Bolt, but Omni was even brighter.

He looked up at the base of the bloom. Was it possible that the gang had passed through this to travel back to earth? He looked at Omni.

"Yes, Bolt," said Omni, "that is the portal through which Mad River Magic passed. And you shall pass through it as well. I hope you will always remember your time here and keep my radio with you. You can always ask me for help. You will hear voices influencing you for good and for evil, voices from the Strata. If you listen closely, one of those voices will be Solia. Take her advice. The other will be Contra. You discovered that my power and love could destroy Extor. Contra has already taken his place. He is my son, and I will not destroy him. But when you hear his voice, know that you should not follow his advice."

Bolt nodded in agreement. There was movement behind Omni. A light gray stratoid stepped out. It was the server from the reception center.

"Someone else wanted to say good-by," said Omni.

Bolt climbed out of his cart and shuffled his feet, not knowing what to say.

The server stepped up to him, putting her hands on his shoulders. A light gray blush glowed from her face. She kissed him on the cheek. "I am proud to have been part of your journey. I will remember you forever. I hope you never forget me."

Bolt cleared his throat and spoke with a husky voice, "Never."

"Okay," said Omni with a chuckle. "It is time for you to catch up with the rest of the gang."

He planted a kiss on the top of Bolt's head, and floated him back into his cart. "God speed, my friend."

The petals parted, revealing a three-leafed aperture. Omni tapped Bolt's cart, and it blasted through the opening, throwing Bolt back against his seat with a force greater than he had experienced on the trip to the Strata.

He felt the same forces of expansion and contraction as he had entering the Strata. But his fear was calmed, knowing that Omni had launched him. He grabbed a big breath, expecting the coming inability to breathe. His cart spun like a rifle bullet. Total silence. Total darkness. A cold blanket of air engulfed him. Then, in half the time of travel to the Strata, he felt the forces of deceleration and heard the same jet engine whine.

He saw a dot of light ahead. Sighing, he found that he could breathe again. The air became warmer. The dot turned into a large multicolored target.

With a final swoosh, his cart plopped into the warm green environment of Cedar Heights.

Bolt climbed out of his cart, surrounded by the rest of the gang. Wheels had reappeared on the carts, and they appeared to be wet. The gang was dressed once again in the clothes they had on when they had entered the Strata. Their pockets bulged with their Omni Radios, wands peeked out of each of their shirts. And they were standing beside the magic pond at the back of the forest. A large Arbor Vitae, the tree of life, near the pond was swaying, water dripping from its branches, even though there was no breeze. The gurgling of the Mad River soothed his anxiety. They were home!

Taking in the green of the trees and the grass, the blue of the pond and the sky, the yellow sunshine, and all the shades of color in between, Bolt took an even bigger breath. Wow, this was a beautiful place.

"How long have you been here?" Bolt asked Rey.

She looked at him with an are-you-okay look. "We just got here, right along with you."

"Okay." He shook his head in disbelief. That was some trip.

"What did you do with Extor?" Rey asked.

"Oh, Omni took care of him," said Bolt. "Actually, Omni destroyed him." He looked around for Mr. Finkelstein.

Sitting up on the metal bed between Bug and Lil's carts, Finkelstein was rubbing his eyes and checking his extremities. He didn't try to stand. He seemed to be in disbelief that he was home, slapping his face repeatedly.

Bolt approached him. "I don't think Extor will be bothering you anymore, Mr. Finkelstein. Omni turned him into a pile of ashes."

Finkelstein tried to stand, but quickly sat down, his weak emaciated legs not able to hold him. Joy filled his eyes, and for the first time ever, Bolt saw a smile spread across his face. Finkelstein grabbed Bolt's hand with both of his.

"Thank you, kind neighbor," Finkelstein said. "Would you take me to my wife?"

Bolt felt a warm glow of purpose for living fill his chest. "Certainly, sir."

"Wait a second," said Rey. "We don't want your wife to see you so weak and skinny." She walked to the Mad River and dipped her wand tip into the magic waters. The Red Cedar tip glowed bright once again. Rey tapped Mr. Finkelstein on his forehead. "*Kiikilo!*"

Finkelstein jerked back as if zapped with electricity. His eyes widened and the sunken look disappeared. His shirt and pants began to fill out as his wiry frame regained its vigor.

Bolt looked at Rey in amazement. "Did you take some private lessons from Omni?"

She grinned and pulled her Omni Radio from her back pocket. "I've got him right here with me, Master Bolt. You better watch out or we'll turn Mr. Finkelstein's Doberman into a cheetah." She waved her wand at him.

Bolt grabbed his Omni Radio from under the dash of his cart. "You forget, Princess Rey, that these wands are to be used for light magic, not dark. You wouldn't want Omni to turn you into a pile of ashes, now would you?"

Steve Hooley

"Come on, kids," interrupted Finkelstein. "Are you going to take me home, or do I have to walk?"

Chapter Thirty

Paradise on Earth

ad River Magic whooped and hollered as they raced their carts through the forest. Wow, it was good to be back in the Cedar Heights world, where the air was sweet and the colors were bright. The trail through the forest had never looked so inviting.

In spite of Finkelstein's requests to slow down, Bug insisted on taking every turn at top speed. Lil clung to her wheel with white knuckles, but Bug pulled them faster as she banked as high and steep as she could, tilting the metal platform between the two carts at a steep angle. Poor Finkelstein hung on as if...well, his life probably did depend on it. Bolt slipped into position beside Bug to get her to slow down. She raised her second and third fingers in a V, and yelled a cheer of victory.

Scout dropped behind, checking on all the new blooms and furry creatures in the Cedar Heights forest. Rey seemed to be carrying on a conversation with Omni. She was probably seeing how far she would be allowed to go with her new power and magic. Bolt groaned.

When they reached the Finkelstein residence, the gang set their carts down on the Cedar Heights side of the fence. Finkelstein jumped from the metal platform before it could lift off again.

The gang watched, standing on their carts and looking over the fence, as Finkelstein rushed around the fence and into his backyard. Dobie greeted him with barking, jumping, and running circles around him.

Mrs. Finkelstein came out the back door onto the deck. "There you are, Henry. Where have you been? You're an hour late for supper."

"You wouldn't believe me if I told you," he answered. He turned and winked at the gang.

"Don't give me any of that other-world stuff you've spouted in the past," said Mrs. Finkelstein. "You've used that line too many times already. What *are* you up to?"

"Actually, I was imprisoned in that other world," he said. "And the neighbor kids rescued me and brought me back."

"Right," she said. "Now get into the house and clean up for supper."

Finkelstein turned to the gang and raised his arms, as if conducting an orchestra. "Watch this," he said, motioning for the gang to rise and fly.

Mad River Magic mounted their carts and zoomed over the fence, circling around the backyard. Bolt couldn't resist buzzing Dobie a few times.

Mrs. Finkelstein swooned, falling back into a patio chair.

Mr. Finkelstein waved and yelled his thanks. "She'll claim that this was just a dream," he called to the gang.

Mad River Magic waved good-bye and headed for the Cedar Heights council house. Bolt hoped Gram was fixing supper, too.

∞ ∞ ∞

A minute later, the gang landed their carts outside the back door and exploded through the patio into the dining area.

"Gram! Gramps!" Everyone was yelling at once.

Gram sprinted out of the kitchen, her pony tail whipping behind her. "There you are. We've been looking for you everywhere. *Where* have you been? Gramps was afraid you fell into that hole in the back of the forest."

She grabbed her grandchildren, including Bolt, pulling them into a group hug. Everyone, except Lil, pulled loose. She clung to Gram tightly.

Gram smiled and planted a kiss on top of Lil's head.

"We did," said Rey, watching Gram for her response.

"What?" asked Gram. She pulled out a chair and sat down. "Now don't play games with me." She looked at each of the gang to see if they were kidding. Then, in shock and disbelief, she yelled, "Honey! Get out here. The kids are back."

Gramps walked out from his office, an ancient book opened in his hand. Rey and Bolt's eyes met.

"Well, it's about time." Gramps hugged each member of the gang, one at a time. "I was about to come looking for you."

"Where were you going to look?" asked Rey.

"That's not important now that you're back." He closed the book and set it on the kitchen table.

Bolt picked up the book and checked the title carefully.

"The kids said they *did* fall into that hole, Honey." Gram turned to Gramps with a worried look. "It's time to find a way to destroy it and fill it in."

"I think Omni has already taken care of that," said Bolt.

"Who is Omni?" asked Gram.

"Wait," said Gramps. "You children sit down and tell us everything."

Two hours later, when the family had finished supper and Mad River Magic had answered all of Gram's and Gramps' questions, Gramps was rubbing his forehead and was deep in thought. He glanced at the old book that now lay on a side table and quietly tucked it under his arm.

Shaking his head and still in disbelief, he addressed the gang. "Now, the out-of-town cousins are showing up next week for the rest of the summer. I don't want you guys to tell them anything about the Strata, your adventures, and especially about the aperture."

"Yeah, right," said Bug, laughing. "Get real, Gramps."

"I'm going to look at that hole," said Gramps. "If it's still there, I'm going to order a whole truckload of dynamite."

"I'm going with you," said Scout, getting up and heading for the door.

"Me, too," said Bug, quickly following.

Lil moved to Gram and hugged her shoulders.

As Bolt stood to follow the look-see in the back of the forest, he noticed Rey trying to tug the book away from Gramps.

He quietly pulled his wand and aimed it at the book. "*Tepeki-shawe*[33]." That should make it easier to find in the future, after Rey hid it.

"Would you guys wait a few minutes while I go see my mom?" asked Bolt. "I'll be right back."

∞ ∞ ∞

Bolt landed the cart in his backyard. He almost wished Jerk had been outside so he could buzz him. Na, he had to stop calling him Jerk. If he could learn to get along with Finkelstein, he could get along with Jack, too...if for nothing more than his mom's sake. It would be tough.

---

[33] Glow in the dark (tay-pay-kee shah-way)

Wow, he couldn't wait to see his mom. He should have gone to see her before going to Cedar Heights. A twinge of guilt stabbed his chest. It seemed like an eternity since he had seen her. The memory of talking to his dad in the mirror, and seeing the pictures of his dad age, gave him a new appreciation of the struggle his mom had silently lived with, trying to give him a decent life. Anyway, he couldn't wait to see her. He stick-hopped in through the back door, catching the door to keep it from banging.

His mom was fixing supper. She looked up with a tired smile. Jack was still in the living room in his favorite spot, in front of the computer.

"Hi, son," she said. "You must have had a good day with the gang. You're late for supper."

"It was different," said Bolt. He gave his mom a big hug and kissed her on the cheek.

She looked at him with surprise, then inspected him from top to bottom. "Something about you looks different. Are you okay?"

"I couldn't be better," he answered with a big smile. Man, it was good to see her again. He needed to do something around here to make her life easier.

"Tell me about your day," she said, stirring the sizzling hamburger in the skillet.

"Well..." he paused. He couldn't tell her. She would worry, or she wouldn't let him roam Cedar Heights anymore. The part about Dad would only sadden her. Oh, this was tough. Maybe that was part of growing up, knowing when to keep your mouth shut, so it wouldn't hurt someone. Ah, it was okay. She was here. He was back. He would be a better son. He sighed and felt the warm glow of satisfaction. "We took an interesting journey through the forest, negotiating the forces of good and evil. It took us awhile to get back."

She turned to him and laughed. "That sounds like quite the intellectual pursuit. And here I thought you were just racing the trails and exploring the forest."

Yeah, it was big, the biggest challenge he had ever faced, mental or physical. He looked down at his crutches. And it was important, too. Why did so many heroes have to hide what they were doing while they were saving the world? He glanced at his legs. They weren't such a handicap after all.

He couldn't wait for the out-of-town cousins to show up. They deserved to go on an adventure, too. Hmm. Somehow he knew that book Gramps had been studying would hold the key to their next journey, and he bet Rey would try to hide it from him. But he had a good idea where that hiding place would be.

"Oh," yelled Bolt, as he headed out the door again, "someone told me that you should look in that old foot locker in the back of the closet...when you're alone."

He paused to keep the door from slamming. The disappointed look on his mom's face brought him to a complete stop. Without closing his eyes, he could see his dad's writing on the mirror. "Remember your mother...she needs you."

After glancing at the stack of dirty dishes in the sink, then looking out the door toward the back of the forest, Bolt sighed and moved toward the dishes. Man, knowing now what he should or shouldn't do only made things more difficult. Oh, for the age of innocence. Or was that ignorance?

He hung his head and muttered under his breath, "Thanks a lot, Omni."

But, halfway through the dishes, the look on his mom's face, mouth hanging open and speechless, was worth it all. And tomorrow would bring another adventure.

Chapter Thirty-One

Shawnee Magic Spells

Shawnee magic spell (pronunciation)	interpretation
Metemyilo! (may-taym-yee-lo)	Follow the path!
Kiikilo! (keee-kee-lo)	Heal!
Manetoowiiyilo! (mah-nay-too-weee-yee-lo)	Take power!
Wa'the'kilo! (wah-thay-kee-lo)	Let there be light!
Weewaawiyaayaaki! (waay-waah-wee-yaah-yaah-kee)	Dance ring!
Wipi! (wee-pee)	Hurry! Quick!
Laaloopikaatilo! (laah-loo-pee-kaah-tee-lo)	Paralyze! - swinging legs

Kchiptilo!   Tie up!
(kcheep-tee-lo)

Tawenehilo!   Unlock!
(tah-way-nay-hee-lo)

Teki!   Stop!
(tay'kee)

Hachthwilo!   Jump!
(hahch-thwee-lo)

Piyalo!   Come!
(pee-yah-lo)

Hayalo!   Go!
(hah-yah-lo)

Hapapilo!   Sit down!
(hah-pah-pee-lo)

Shekwe!   Gum!
(shay-kway)

Honthe'lo!   Fly!
(hon-they-lo)

Chaki tekhaaka!   small ax, tomahawk!
(chak-kee tayk-haah-kay)

Tehashichtheto!   Paste!
(tay-hah-sheech-thay-to)

Tepika!   Measure!
(tay-pee-kah)

Neekata!   Follow!
(naay-kah-tah)

Mshikanwi!   Wind!
(mshee-kah-nwee)

Kekilshimthoothwa!   Buffalo bull!
(kay-keel-shee-m-thoo-thwah)

Nenekilo!   Pulverize!
(nay-nay-kee-lo)

Pemhanwi!   It floats!
(paym-hah-nwee)

Kithilo!   Wash!
(kee-thee-lo)

Hakwichinwi!   Float it!
(hah-kwee-chee-nwee)

Wiiwiil'shkwa!   Glue!
(weee-weeel-shkwah)

Chaakatethilo!   Burn up!
(chaah-kah-tay-thee-lo)

Pkwahilo!   Break off!
(pkwah-hee-lo)

Hatchi kiishoowenaki! Moving pictures
(hah-tchee keee-shoo-way-nah-kee)

Sooshkilo!   Straighten!
(shoosh-kee-lo)

Pkaleshkote!   Blazing fire!
(pkah-lay-shko-tay)

Nimachilota!   I destroy it!
(nee-mah-chee-lo-tah)

Tepeki-shawe!   Glow in the dark!
(tay-pay-kee shah-way)

<<<<>>>>

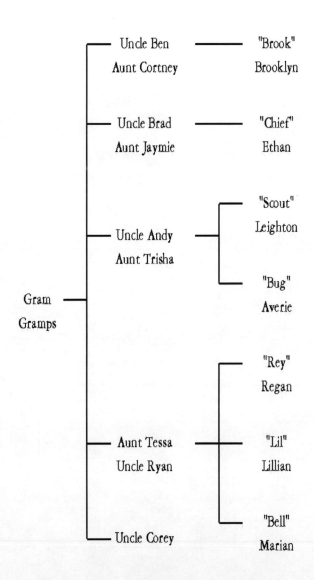

	Uncle Ben	"Brook"
	Aunt Cortney	Brooklyn
	Uncle Brad	"Chief"
	Aunt Jaymie	Ethan
	Uncle Andy	"Scout"
	Aunt Trisha	Leighton
Gram		"Bug"
Gramps		Averie
		"Rey"
		Regan
	Aunt Tessa	"Lil"
	Uncle Ryan	Lillian
		"Bell"
	Uncle Corey	Marian

Mad River Magic Cousins

Maps

THE FOLLOWING TWO PAGES:

Mad River Magic's world – Cedar Heights

The   Strata

Omni's Mountain

Sdia's Palace of Light

The Omniflex Tunnel

The Hemlock Forest

The Hemlock River

The Desert of Indecision

Extor's Palace of Night

Contra's Cavern

Omni's Aperture

The Hemlock Aperture

The Strata

About the author

Steve Hooley is a physician/writer living in rural western Ohio, the setting for the Mad River Magic series. He and his wife have five children and seven grandchildren, who have inspired his stories.

The author invites you to visit his website:

www.SteveHooleyWriter.com

where you can sign up for his newsletters and be the first to be notified of new book releases or special deals.

Steve Hooley

Made in the USA
Middletown, DE
15 May 2019